FAITHFUL
JENNY DOVE

FAITHFUL JENNY DOVE

And Other Tales

by

ELEANOR FARJEON
(1881- 1965)

Short Story Index Reprint Series

 BOOKS FOR LIBRARIES PRESS
FREEPORT, NEW YORK

Frst Published 1925
Reprinted 1970

INTERNATIONAL STANDARD BOOK NUMBER:
0-8369-3625-6

LIBRARY OF CONGRESS CATALOG CARD NUMBER:
78-128734

PRINTED IN THE UNITED STATES OF AMERICA

To COLA

CONTENTS

	PAGE
"——AND A PERLE IN THE MYDDES"	1
"THE SHEPHEARD'S GYRLOND"	63
FAITHFUL JENNY DOVE	107
THE LAMB OF CHINON	139
THE TOMBOLA	157
THE RED APPLES	189
FIRING THE RUSH	209
ANNA	235

"——AND A PERLE IN THE MYDDES"

I

"*TOM! hi, Tom! Tom Thacker!*"

Snowballs belong to the category of the unexpected. Even on the dark of a December afternoon, when earth is white and schools are emptied, their essential quality is still that of surprise. A rear attack, and cold shrapnel down the collar . . . no amount of snow on the ground and riotous boyhood in the streets can eliminate the factor of shock from this, of all things unexpected the most, in the conditions, to be expected.

In the streets, I say. But when to the winter-dark is superadded the gloom of a dimly lit cathedral, where, of all things expected, snowballs, even on a snowy winter's day, must surely be the least! . . .

"*Tom Thacker! Tom, I say!*"

Then the shot and the shudder.
Or did the shudder precede the shock. Certainly

a shuddering of the soul possessed me at hearing my own name uttered in that ghostly atmosphere where I, the victim of an ill-organised train-service, was a chance and absolute stranger. Swift on the spiritual shivering followed the bodily. I turned sharply. A little shadow seemed to waver behind a pillar, a stifled giggle to flicker in the gloom. At an appreciable distance an ancient verger pottered among the monuments of the great dead. He solely shared my solitude. His face was like puckered parchment. One could not suspect such dry dust capable of the melting onslaught. Besides, I had had speech with him, and he had tasted silver.

Considering my position tactically, I turned my back upon the pillar, the ambush, I now felt assured, of something which had haunted me from the hour of my birth. And longer ; but I did not at the moment realise this in its full significance. I did, however, realise that what the pillar concealed had compelled and eluded me since my descent on Welchester platform three hours previously, where I was told that my earliest connection with Bridestow was at 10.25 before midnight—a slow train landing me at my goal at four o'clock in the morning.

I was joining the house-warming of one of my oldest friends, five miles outside Bridestow ;

my invitation extended over a month's span, and covered Christmas and Twelfth-Night festivities. December the sixth saw me stranded in an unknown town with that strange sense of joylessness which accompanies the going agley of journey-plans in a chilly dusk. But something more than the customary forlornness was needed to account for my mood.

A kind of fatality, a premonition of unseen forces at work, deepened it to a significance hardly communicable in words. I was not experiencing this for the first time, but I had never before experienced it in such an acute degree. The sensation itself recurred annually, lasting the greater part of each December. A desperate unrest possessed me, an unaccountable certainty that I was wanted Somewhere by Someone. At intervals I had the feeling that I was wanted less in another place than in another era. The distances of time rather than space dragged at the roots of me. My complete ignorance of the cause of this periodical mood rendered me incapable of dispelling it; but no December within my memory had passed without the return of the disturbance, and I knew that if its motive-power were ever made plain to me by some clue of chance, I would obey it to the limits of unreason.

To outsiders my spiritual disease in this period was made accountable by a physical ailment which succeeded to the mood with a clockwork regularity. So surely as Christmas Day began to lengthen its shadows, so surely was I beset with a violent ague. Fever and shivering battled for possession of my body during some seven days, and expired together, leaving me a weak and despondent victor. The yearly recurrence of this illness was in itself something of a mystery; but it served ostensibly to justify the three-weeks' moodiness of which it was the apparent culmination. Yet inwardly I knew my mental disorder to be a thing in nowise dependent on the bodily affliction it preceded.

On the morning of my departure for Bridestow, I was still unaffected by my annual gloom; I had commenced my journey in sunlight, free of any psychic trouble; but very soon the cloud began to gather and grow dense, and at Welchester, where my train branched off from the Bridestow line, it was of an extraordinary oppressiveness. Even had the train been continuing to my destination, I knew that I would still have been compelled to alight at this place. On the platform, my baggage about me, I discovered the alteration of the train I had relied on to carry me to my friends that night. The prospect of the 10.25 was impossibly cheerless ; of course, I would spend the night in Welchester. But even without the warranting circumstances, I knew that I *must*. Something in Welchester wanted me.

Should he, said the porter, carry my things to the Station Hotel? It seemed the reasonable course ; but I shook my head, and had them deposited in the parcels office. I had a premonition that I would not be sleeping at the Station Hotel that night.

I turned out into the streets, where pale early lamplight and dingy daylight struggled feebly with the mirage of light cast upward by the snow.

I told myself I must get something to eat, and made an unhesitating track through the streets of the dim old city. I had heard much of the historic and romantic charm of Welchester, but I scarcely looked about me as I went. For I began to realise that I knew the charm and the city by heart. I had trod these ways before. I barely heard the sound of my own steps on the powdered pavements. It was as though they were trodden by a ghost.

I came to halt. Not before hotel, or restaurant, or tea-shop—*that* had not been the primitive need directing me ; but in front of the grand

Cathedral towering in ancient silence on the city's marge. Beyond it stretched flat quiet fields, level with the frozen Wele, which holds the old cathedral town in a crook of its arm like a lover. One of these flats was dotted with gravestones; on another boys were playing, their voices and scufflings coming with an odd effect of being more far-off than they were. Some of them were sliding on the river, or chucking stones and lumps of broken ice across its slippery face. At yet a little distance the great fragments of Welchester Castle stood out against the sky. A dull glow from the west filtering through the ruined windows lit them into a semblance of life. It seemed possible to imagine men and women still habiting those windy chambers; and boys, boys. . . .

"What do you want?"

I uttered the words aloud, in mechanical answer to a thin sound in the air seeming to call my name—to a wisp of motion plucking at my sleeve. But I was mistaken; it had been a trick of the wind.

As I turned into the Cathedral the rumour of the great organ flooded me; then, sweet and shrill, the voices of choir-boys. Some service or practice was on. Disappointed, I turned away. I wanted the place to myself. All these others—worshippers, choristers, priests, had no business there. I must bide my time.

At the door I heard—did I hear?—the merest whisper.

"*Tom* . . ."

I paused, breath held. I looked back. Uncertain shadows danced about me.

"Imagination," I decided; "I'll get something to eat and come back again." And I repeated, not in my thoughts, but under my breath, like an assurance: "I shall come back again."

I made a tour of the great building, turning my back on the west where the country stretched into the open. Streets lay to the east, and shops, too, I supposed, for by an angle of the east wall I heard the clinking of an anvil.

"There'll be a bakery near the smithy," I remembered, and turned the corner. But there was no smithy, only another angle of the Cathedral wall, an unfamiliar angle that protruded itself like an impertinence upon me who knew by heart each stone of this beloved building.

I could no longer hear the sound of iron on iron, but I had come right for the shops, of a sort. Little, mean, crooked streets like crippled beggar children huddled for warmth under this aspect of the Cathedral. I turned down the nearest, an ill-lit alley, crowded with poor shop-fronts, at the door of one of which a figure was standing. I quickened my step, and she moved instantly to meet me, hands outstretched a little, such a small, frail slip of a thing; until she was quite close I was certain she was a girl-child, and then I saw her for a bent old woman. She came to an abrupt stop as our eyes met, and hers were dim and startled.

"I beg your pardon, my dear," she said in a bewildered voice.

She was a very sweet old lady.

"Where can I get a cup of tea, mother?"

"Will you come in?" She indicated her shop-door, above which the sign "M. Venn" was just readable in half-obliterated paint.

"Is that your name?" I had an obscure feeling that there was some mistake.

"Yes, sir." She was recovering from whatever had troubled her in our encounter.

I entered the little shop. It was shabby, but exceedingly clean. Behind the counter, where loaves and cakes were sold, was entrance to a tiny parlour. Here she served me at a ridiculous price; she ran out for eggs and fresh butter, and a rasher of ham, and laid the bills rather shyly beside my plate as being no part of her concern; she held herself responsible only for the tea, the brown rolls, and the really delicious home-made cake. She waited on me tremulously. We said very little. As I rose to go she asked,

"Was it all right, my dear?"

I assured her it was. It was as much as I could do not to kiss her. There were tears in her eyes, and the same trouble seemed to stir in her that I had noticed at first. Her two old hands strayed out as though to keep me. I was reluctant to go; yet one other call was stronger in me.

"Good-evening——" I hesitated, glanced at her left hand, and added, "Mrs. Fenn." To which she answered in a subdued way: "Good-evening, sir," and coloured faintly, and hid her wedding-ring beneath her apron.

When I turned at the end of the mean little street, she was still at her door.

People were streaming out of the Cathedral now, and for a little while I loitered about the big graveyard. Many of the tombs were old out of knowledge. In a remote corner a couple of graves had been recently dug up; ancient tenants were to be displaced by new. Their crumbling headstones lay propped against a bank.

One could not read the dates and inscriptions upon them: the weather had read them too often, had worn the pages blank.

I turned into the Cathedral.

The verger was there and, confound them, a few visitors. A stupid hour for visitors, cried my impatient soul; what could they hope to see in this light? Later I judged them to be American tourists "rushing" Great Britain, each half-hour planned in advance. Welchester's allotted morsel fell unfortunately; but the Cathedral is one of England's sights, and one could always say, you know, that one had not missed it.

The verger was telling things to his party. I walked towards them, not because I wished to hear, but because they were centred round the precise spot in that vast and beautiful building where my heart was beating.

"See here, Helen—the *cunnin'* mite!"

"Oh, the cutey! Who is he, anyway?"

"I guess he's that baby priest thing Mr. Levant told us be sure not to miss—now where is it?"

She turned to the inevitable Baedeker, but Master Verger was before her, a lean finger on the tiny stone effigy that was the momentary point of curiosity.

The Boy-Bishop has slipped from the memory —which means from the heart—of a world that needs him no more. Bluff King Hal struck him a buffet ; Mary resuscitated him ; and Queen Bess killed him for good. But for years, numbering their hundreds, there was no choir attached to the Church or the private chapels of the nobility that did not each December elect its mimic Bishop, whose term of office lasted from Saint Nicholas to Childermas. He had his trappings, his dignities, his parades ; such authority as the Bishop exercised in the world of clerics was his above his youthful comrades ; he even preached to them in the great Cathedral. It was a three-weeks' festival this of the Boy-Bishop, with enough of pageantry and quaint licence to make it attractive to the boyish troop it concerned : a child's mummery, smiled on and sanctioned by Mother Church, who doubtless derived her own benefit therefrom. It was said that if the little chosen chorister died while still bearing his honours, he was buried with the full dignities of his estate. Some antiquaries have disputed this point ; but in the Cathedrals of Welchester and Salisbury tiny child-effigies bear out the truth of it. No visible inscription supported the claims of the little figure our verger droned of ; but here he was, a child in the midst of four great monuments bearing the names of princes of the Church—historic names.

"And what do you believe?" one of the fair Americans attacked her guide.

He coughed dustily. "It may be so, miss, and it may *not* be so. They do say there are other heffigies cast in a minute mould to be seen elsewhere—such as knights and what not, full-grown men, you understand me, but carved smallish for convenience as it were. However, there it is."

Yes, there it was, old sceptic. How else could this small accident have crept in among those stately prelates but as their brother? A flash of ridiculous wrath passed through me. It was on the tip of my tongue to tell them all about it . . . but about what? Ah, it was on the tip of my tongue, on the giddy verge of memory. I could no more grasp it than I could grasp that shadow dancing so oddly behind one of the great tombs.

"But don't you know his name? He must at least have a name!" the lady persisted.

"We have no evidence to that effect, miss," returned the verger with dry precision. "We possess the hinventory of his vestments, however. The register lies opened under the glass case to your right. The character of the 'andwriting is Gothic, and somewhat 'ard to decipher. They had no Schoolboard in those days, miss." He paused a moment for the slight but inevitable snigger of appreciation, cleared his throat a little, and ran over the list in his guide's monotone, without glancing at the protected parchment. My eye travelled down that antique document with ease. . . .

"*Imprimis*, myter well garnished with perle and precious stones, with nowches of silver, and gilt before and behind.

"*Item*, iiij rynges of silver and gilt with four redde precious stones in them.

"*Item*, j pontifical with silver and gilt, with a blew stone in hytt.

"*Item*, j owche broken silver and gilt, with iiij precious stones and a perle in the myddes——"

"They appear not to have considered pearls as precious stones," one of the young ladies observed.

"Them was the days of ignorance and darkness, miss; we know better now.—*Item*, a Crosse with a staf of coper and gilt . . . a vesture redde with lyons of silver and brydds of gold . . . one albe to the same with stars in the paro (that's the same as to say the apparel, miss) . . . one tabard of skarlett and a hoode thereto . . . one stayned cloth of the ymage of Saint Nicholas . . . ."

So he went on. And through his professional drone I repeated in my heart: "We know better now, we know better now."

"What a trousseau!" "Helen" was speaking. "But I wish I knew his name."

"You wouldn't be much the wiser for it, miss." Master Verger evidently resented the implication of his own ignorance. "We now pass on to the Grinling Gibbons Screen, carved in the year—"

He meandered to some other glory of the Cathedral. Its beauties were barely visible by night, and his little tribe followed eagerly. I stepped across Miss Helen's shadow as she passed. For the life of me I could not help it.

"His name, madam," I said, "was Nicholas Cope."

She eyed me in faint astonishment. "Oh, thank you; that's very interesting." Acknowledging me with a bow, she passed on, puzzled.

Yet less so than myself. Why had I said that? How did I know. But I did know.

"*Tom!* . . . *Tom* . . ." breathed the elusive whisper that was one with the elusive shadow. I slipped behind the tomb; but it was too quick for me.

IN THE MYDDES" 17

The verger looked back, expectant of me. I approached and put a half-crown into his palm.

"I'll wander round by myself a bit; I know this place."

"That will be quite as you please, sir, I am sure." This was he at his most affable. I dropped the party and went in chase of my shadow. I had not lied. I knew the place, though I had never set foot in it in my life.

My shadow had vanished. It was playing hide-and-seek with me. I felt the jolly little soul of mischief in the atmosphere.

"You shan't escape me," I muttered. "I'll get hold of you somehow. . . ."

The droning voice wandered farther off, farther. The party took leave. Through a high window I saw stars on a frosty sky. Inside the Cathedral the light was very dim.

"*Tom! hi, Tom! Tom Thacker!*"

There was my name in full, confessed. My shadow knew me. I would know him or die. The verger was approaching slowly.

"*Tom Thacker! Tom, I say!*"

And then! the villainous snowball full in

the nape, and the darting shadow to the column's shelter, and the muffled laughter. . . .

This was the moment for manœuvres. And I, as I have said, turned my back on the certainty of that concealing column, and loitered in a wide careless circle until I had gained the right side of it, back still turned. But my unconscious ally, the verger, guarded the other side, and I had my prisoner between two fires. I leapt round and was on him—on whatever the column had been hiding.

"Now then, you young beggar!" I breathed in a triumphant whisper.

And it was no shadow—or was it? ah, but none to me! Two quick young hands were up about my neck, an eager cheek was pressed against mine, and the answering whisper was half a sob, half a laugh.

"Tom! Tom! *dear* old Tom! I knew thou'ldst come this year."

"Nick!" I said. And for the first time I began to have a glimmer of the need that had drawn me to Welchester, that had been drawing me back since the day, centuries past, when Nicholas Cope died during his term of office.

The verger was close upon us.

"Look slippy!" said Nick. Hugging my arm he dragged me away, out of the holy shadow into the holy starlight. The snow crisped under our shoes. Nick looked up, a grin all over his jolly freckled little face.

"Say, old Tom, I got thee a good 'un, did not I?"

II

I LOOKED down at the sturdy boyish form trudging beside me in the hose and jerkin of the fifteenth century.

"Yes," I assented, "you got me a good 'un. And now, you young beggar, we'll have this out. Who are you?"

"Who I be?" ejaculated he. "Dostna know me? Thou rotter!" He executed a little caper under the stars. "Oh, Tom, isna this snow just *bully*!"

"Hold hard!" I said. "Where did you pick up this stuff? Surely this wasn't your fashion of talk?"

"No, beshrew me!" laughed Nicholas Cope. "Thou and I were wont to mangle speech in other wise, ha, Tom? Dost remember how old Withun would rate us? 'Murtherers o' the honest Saxon!' a' called us. (I loved him, though.) But Lord! the kind worms they do eat holes even in my old stones within yonder, and so I hear what I hear. I'll tell thee what I know, shall I ? 'Corking' and 'lemon' I know, and 'skidoo' and 'cute'— why, I be called cute a dozen times a day o' Junes, Tom."

"These are all Americanisms," I said.

"Very like. It be a friendly talk to hear in one's lonesomeness."

"Are you very lonely, Nick?"

"Oh, Tom! . . . an I'd but lived two days longer I'd ha' been buried among the children."

"Poor old chap."

"Out here— " we were crossing the grave-yard now—" it be jolly at all seasons. Earth she's a kind guardian, a' be full o' cracks. Can hear the birds sing, and boys a-quarrel, can watch the roots o' things and little live beasts, ha ? Oh, but within there, all amid those four stern preachers, that lie so strait and pompified from March to February! 'tis, 'Peace, peace, thou restless imp!' if one but turn to ease a cramp. I would I hadna died a bishop, Tom."

"Never mind, Nick. Here you are, escaped."

"Ay. This is my holy-day. Three weeks, and thou, and the snow all together! isna it jolly ?"

"Nick," I said, "who was I ?"

"Lord, what small memories men have,"

said he wistfully. "I did think thee jesting a while back. Dost truly not remember?"

"No facts, Nick. Only that we loved each other."

"That be fact enough, I guess. I'll mind thee of the rest. Oh, we've days before us! Thou wert my younger when I died, and now, ha, ha! Tom's got hair on's face. Thou dost look odd i' thy beard, Tom! Is't a fearful bore to clip and trim? I warrant it be sport—I would I had lived beard-long. Wilt let me see thee at Master Barber's, Tom?"

"But Master Barber will see you too."

"Nay, only thou. Others be so blind, they canna see me; and numb, they canna touch me; and deaf, not to hear me."

"And why am I not blind and numb and deaf to thee, Nick?"

My hand was lifted to a warm mouth.

"We loved each other," answered Nicholas Cope.

III

"Where are we for, old fellow?" I asked.

"We be for seeking my owche," said Nick soberly. "I lost it, dostna remember? *Thou* shouldstna ha' forgotten that, Tom. Thou'lt help me, wilt thou? I must find my owche—I *must*." He gave a little sigh.

"Why, Nick?"

"They say I shallna sleep in peace till it be found again. The sin's a shadow on my immortal soul, they say. And so year by year I must walk, and go a-looking for my owche." He sighed again, then kicked up his heels and grinned out of the corner of mouth and eye. "Silly asses? who wants to sleep in peace? Us was ever cutting capers o' nights when old Withun wasna spying. Tom!" he wheedled my hand. "Thou'lt bide past Yule and go treasure-hunting, ha? Great nights we'll have, and none to say us nay. Thou'lt bide, Tom?"

"To the death, Nick!"

"Ay," he said softly. "bide till then."

"I'll find a hotel near the Cathedral, if there is one."

"Oh, no, Tom, not an hostel. Bide with Marget."

"Marget?"

"Ay, Marget of the bakery, her that was Marget Catton, and then was Marget Fenn. (But that was after *my* time.) Oh, thou hastna forgotten Marget the Smithy's daughter?—

Tom, thou *art* a rotter! And thou and she so jolly thick—she liked thee best of the bunch of us, and we all so keen on her as we were. Come, Tom, think, Tom! I punched the heads of half the choir for thy sake because they were mad about thee and her, and—thou wastna *very* spry at punching heads thyself, Tom."

"Thank you, Nick. And weren't you keen on Marget, too?"

"Oh, well . . . pretty keen. But I loved thee best, and so did she."

"And after all the baggage went and married this Fenn chap, confound him."

"Thou mustna miscall young Matt, Tom. I couldna ha' got thee out o' the water without him, not for all the little Princeling's help, and Geoffrey Appsley had made himself scarce, the dirty funk."

"Well, if I owe young Matt my life, I suppose I must forgive him Marget. How came I in the water, and what was the Princeling doing there?"

"Lord, what wasna he!" Nick chuckled. "A nice mess that was for all of us, and if Geoffrey had but taken his licking like a man——! The Prince was no funk, nay, it wasna Ned's fault."

"You've still left me in mid-water, Nick,"

I said patiently. "I'll go under without a helping hand."

"That's where Matt o' the Fenn comes in; and so we'll to Marget's, because 'tis closing time. Keep thy hair on; I'll mind thee of everything afore the bells ring in the Christ. Race thee to Marget's, Tom Thacker!"

He bounded away, shouting and tossing back his hood, a boy out of school, primed for games and mischief. And I—raced after him, and so we arrived in breathless laughter at the little bakery where I had supped, and Nick pommelled on the door, and I clouted him over the ear and knocked decorously. Margaret Venn opened to us, and inquiry changed to welcome in her old eyes as they met mine. Of Nick dancing on the step, and snuffing up the scent of crust and cake in an ecstasy, she took no note.

"Mrs. Fenn—Venn," (I corrected myself), "I shall be staying in Welchester a few weeks. If you have a room to spare, would you care to take a lodger?"

"Oh, yes, sir!" The soft face brightened. "I have a room—it isn't a very big one—perhaps you wouldn't——? Will you come in and look at it?"

"No, Mrs. Venn, I will not. I'll be stepping up to the station for my traps."

IN THE MYDDES."

"I am not very used——" she faltered.

I took her hand in mine by way of encouragement. "Don't worry, mother. I won't be a trouble to you."

"Oh, it isn't that, sir!"

We left her in a bewildered tremor of doubt and joy.

"Stations be great sport," observed Nick, trotting beside me in profound satisfaction. "An I'd my way over again I wouldna sing i' the choir, I'd be 'prentice to a driver of engines, ay, and I'd keep my throat shut lest they impressed me, as they did thee."

"Me? What did I find so impressive about 'em, whoever they were?"

"Now thou'rt talking gabble. *Impressed* thee, I said."

"And impressed me, I heard. So comb out the tangles."

Nick groaned and rolled his eyes. "Thou canstna help being a dunderhead, old Tom. But for all that thou hadst the sweetest voice in the choir, and if thou didna want to be impressed in my Lord Bishop's service thou shouldst ha' kept thy throat shut i' the lanes and left the birds to their singing. Well! what a mess o' tears and trouble thou wast when they brought thee into the Castle court afront of a rider on a big horse. 'Here be a nightingale to house wi' the thrushes,' a' said ; and they fetched Hugh Withun along, and thou didst sob and sob and call on thy mother. Dostna remember how the boys then about mocked at thee, the little brutes, and old Withun slashed out at 'em and said in his sharp cross voice : 'Tune up,' a' said, 'tune up !' And thou didst only sob louder, crying, 'Mother, mother, mother !' 'That's no nightingale song,' a' said. And thou, ''Tis all the song thou'lt have o' me !' And thou and he did ever after hate most heartily, and yet I loved ye both."

"Did *you* mock at me that day, Nick ?"

His eyes flashed. "Never I ! Never ! Dostna remember, Tom, I gave them bloody noses when they were cruel to thee, because thou wast so pitiful and never a strong one, and I was tough as Withun's shoe-sole. (*We* know how tough that was, eh ?) And, Tom, I took thee into my bed that night when thou wast shaking so quietly i' the dark, lest the other lads heard thee." His underlip quivered a little. "I thought perhaps thou'ldst ha' remembered *that*, Tom . . . I told thee to take comfort. ''Tisna bad here,' I told thee, 'and I'll be thy friend,' I said. And thou didst ask my name, and tell me thine, and so fell asleep."

I slipped an arm about his shoulder. "Don't

grieve at my poor memory, Nick. The big thing has remained alive between us these four hundred years and more."

"And oh, I've been a-weary for thy coming," whispered he.

IV

I HAD the whole story on the following evening, as we sat together in the broken arch of the great window that had once lighted the banqueting-hall of the Lord Bishops of Welchester. Among the crumbled chambers laid open to the air owls flew and hooted like awakened spirits. They and my little Ghost who sat dangling his heels over the broken ledge fifty feet above the earth, seemed to me the only real things in the world ;. the boys once more sliding and tussling on the frozen river in the distance became like ghosts of future ages—and yet, something in their calling voices rang with an echo out of the past. . . . Nick at my side nodded.

"Ay, shut thy eyes, and it might be our fellows again," said he. "Gregory, and Walter, and Ambrose, and all. Though 'twasna often old Withun would let us abroad to do as we pleased. A' kept our noses pretty close to our tasks, and when 'twasna book-learning it was Ut-Re-Mi till our throats ached. This was the time of holy-day for us boys, though, and December was a jolly month from Saint Nick to Holy Innocents."

"Hoo! hoo! hoo!" A white owl whirred past our ears.

"Who? Who? Who?" mocked Nick. "So the boys cried that Saint Nicholas Eve afore I got my bishop's gloves. Gregory hankered for 'em, and might have had 'em for me. Little enow *I* was cut out for a Churchman, Tom! but I was the elder, and the leader in the choir (though none of us had *thy* alto), and Hugh Withun liked me, Lord knows why, for I would plague out his life seven times in a sennight. A' read me a lesson on my responsibilities when they dressed me up in my fine vestments. 'Bethink thee, Nick,' says he, 'thy fellows look to thee for ensample this three weeks, thy person is become as sacred as our Lord Bishop's own, and thou shalt officiate in the Church, and say a Mass on Holy Innocents ; and so thou must forget thy boy's body which is too prone to the frivolities of this world, and remember only thy immortal soul of which it is the rude casket. No pranks, Nick Cope, no pranks for thy credit's sake and mine.' 'I warrant thee, Withun!' says I, and poked at him with my crozier. Up goes his hand, itching for me. 'And leave my sacred person in peace," says I; ''tisna for such as thee to scourge it this three weeks!' And I strutted up and down mightily pleased with my grand clothes, my mitre, and my rings, and my owche, and the alb and tabard worked in gold and blue and scarlet. A' shook his bony finger in my face, and says he, 'As ye will, Master Nick, but if thou do not prune thy manners, or if I catch thee running round the streets in thy episcopal gloves, or if thou be lax in school or choir (for all thy Bishopric), by so much as the winking of an eyelid—I will lay up such a leathering for thee *after* Holy Innocents as thou shalt remember me by to the end of thy days!' Thereat I laughed outright, for he had me fairly, and he did his best not to smile o' one side of his old puckered mouth, and says soberly, 'And now, whom wilt thou elect amongst thy fellows to be thy ministers this three weeks?' 'Tom Thacker shall swing the censer,' says I, and went on to name what others I would have, but there was no more smiles in him after that word."

"From the beginning he was jealous of your love for me," I murmured. A thousand tiny chambers in my heart were unsealing themselves as Nicholas spoke.

"If it was so," said Nick, "what a folly! A boy doesna love another boy and an old man in the same wise. Howbeit, thou wert my censer-swinger, and ever stood nighest me in all the jolly time that followed. Dost remember the procession to the Cathedral yonder for Vespers on Saint Nicholas, us all decked out so fine? and afterwards parading through the town from house to house, getting of monies in the name of Mother Church? and how—ha, ha!—I blessed them that gave liberally? and how we first knocked up the smithy that stood well-nigh in the Cathedral's self along the eastern wall, so that we boys would listen for the stroke on the anvil during choir-practice, and think on Marget instead of our parts——"

"Yes, yes! what happened to the smithy, Nick?"

"They reclaimed it nigh two hundred years ago; it had been holy ground once, but fallen to ruins in *our* times, and the Lord Bishops got rents for it from traders and craftsmen and such; and later on *they* went, and the east aisle was restored. I miss the clang o' the hammer lying in my tomb eleven months o' the year. . . . Well, then, dost remember how Marget Catton came out o' the forge and ran alongside on the cobbles, with eyes for none but thee in thy new alb? and how Matt o' the Fenn laughed out at us when we came to his father, the baker's, and said: 'No man shall ever trap *me* in the livery o' the Church!' and his father said grimly: 'Yet thou shalt come to a baker's cap for all thy wild ways'; and a' doled us a mean bounty wi' the left hand, whereas Catton, the big smith, had given us freely with the right. (So 'twas a stingy blessing Master Baker had o' Nicholas Cope!) And dost remember how well we were supped in the Canon's room?—I had a choice of six of ye to eat with me, and thou, be sure, wast there—white bread and cider, we had, and meat and cheese. Um, um! And the junketings and entertainments to follow! 'twas a rare season for us lads, and Yule to crown it all.

"But little notion had we of the festival time that Yule was to be. For all suddenly, when my term was nigh spent, and I was stuck half the day conning the sermon they had writ for me to speak on Holy Innocents (stupid stuff, not such as I'd ha' preached out o' mine own mouth), came runners and riders to acquaint my Lord Bishop, a' was a good Yorkist, of the approach of who but Prince Edward and his uncle Earl Rivers, then northward bound for

Ludlow Castle. And they were minded to bide in Welchester over Yule, at my Lord Bishop's entertainment. The to-do there was in kitchen and buttery and still-room! and the buzz and flutter among us lads. For we knew naught of the Princeling, save that he was a boy even as ourselves, and it set our tongues clacking and our brains a-wondering. Gregory thought young Ned would have naught to do wi' the likes of us. 'Princes may not herd wi' choir-boys,' said he. 'But they may with God's chosen,' cries Ambrose, his eyes all shining, as his way was when he spoke of the Church; 'they may wi' bishops!' and so nodded at me, sitting over my page, my head between my hands. 'Nick's teeth 'ld chatter in his silly pate if he had but to say God-den to the Prince!' scoffs Gregory, to draw me; and cries I, ''Twould take more than a prince to make *my* teeth chatter; I'm afeard of no twelve-years' boy alive. If I do not get some sport wi' young Ned I'll swallow my sermon.' 'Thou'rt liker to swallow it an thou *dost*,' says Gregory, 'and be swallowed thyself by old Withun to boot; and what Mass we sing o' Holy Innocents 'ill be for mercy o' thy soul, I think!' I've wondered since if Gregory called that speech to mind in after days.

"Well, ere Christ's Eve went out, my Earl

Rivers came in wi' his train and Prince Ned and Geoffrey Appsley—a disgrace to the post of whipping-boy, that one!"

"Whipping-boy, Nick?"

"Ay. Art in a new trouble, Tom?"

"Till Master Appsley's post is made plain."

"Why, why! doesna there be whipping-boys in these days?" demanded Nick curiously. "Your princelings still be flesh and blood, I suppose? What happens when they get 'emselves into hot water?"

"They probably scald."

"Well, well, and well!" Nicholas scratched his pate and pondered the matter. "Yet it sounds fair enow. So they take their own leatherings for their own misdeeds, eh?"

"Why not?"

"*Princes*, Tom! The world's grown hardy. But it sounds fair, ay, it does. Why, in our day the princelings had their whipping-boys, that took their punishment for 'em when they had done this, that, or t'other and needed their souls purged; and Geoffrey Appsley was young Ned's deputy to cheat the devil. A great tough beast, and a clinking coward to boot.

"We didna have more than a glimpse of the Prince that day as he sat at supper (they served it in public against custom, because o' the

season and the occasion), and we boys sang i'
the gallery the while—look how 'tis broken
away yonder, Tom. But he seemed a merry
young cock, and we liked the looks o' him. A'
laughed outright at the subtlety the cook had
devised in his honour, his own figure done as
natural as life in painted jellies so as to make a
boy's mouth water. 'I hope I taste as handsome
as I do smell and look, my Lord!' a' cries; and
our master answers, 'Y'are of the savour
England loves above all others, my Prince.'
'Yet the red rose smells stronger,' says Ned
saucily, and my Lord Bishop, in a stern loud voice,
'The red rose is dead and its roots are withered
in this land.' (And the land smelled Tudor,
Tom, not ten years later, ha?) There was
mummers and dancing fools come after the feast,
but us lads was packed off to bed betimes, and
I lay cudgelling my wits for a way of getting
at the Prince on the morrow.

"Yule o' course was brimmed from sun-up
to sun-down wi' Masses, and banquets, and
frolick, and what not; but there came an hour
after noon when all the bustle was left to the
underlings, and the great ones slept off the dinner
they had sat at from ten till one o' the clock,
and we boys were left to our devices—a rest-
time, said Hugh Withun, because we had a

little Mystery to perform before the Earl when supper was done. And it was in this hour Gregory scampered among us crying : ' Now's the time, Nick, to make good thy vaunt ! They say in the buttery the Prince is shut into his chamber even as we, so fetch him out and we'll see what stuff he's made of.' I saw Gregory thought I dared not, but, ' Bide a bit ! ' I said, and I got into the full glory of my bishop's vestments, and even then I remember as thou pinned on the owche wi' the four bright stones and the pearl i' the middle, thou didst say, ' How ill this catches, Nick.' ' 'Twill serve,' I said, impatient to be gone. ' Be'st going *so* ? ' asked Gregory, and I told him, ' Ay,' for it was my notion I'd be stayed less i' the corridors if I met wi' any of the serving-folk, who had a big respect for my mitre, and none at all for my hood. ' Now,' says I, ' who will follow Daniel into the den of the lion, for only the brave deserves the sport.' And one after another hung back, and thou alone stood by me, saying, ' I'll go where thou leadest, Nick—and Nick,' thou whispered, ' let's go play after on the ice ? ' So I got our necessaries, and we crept away through the empty passages and down the little secret stair that gave on a postern in the menials' quarters. 'Twas a foul day without, dark drew early in, and that befriended us as we stole about the Castle wall. Erelong we were flinging lumps of snow at the window we knew to be the Princeling's. It fetched him swiftly; out comes his head and 'Who's below?' a' calls. '*Pax vobiscum!*' I pronounces, ''tis the Bishop's self.' He stares a little through the mirk, and then 'Thou imp!' a' splutters, and calls over's shoulder, 'Geoffrey, hi, 'tis the Child-Bishop come to give us a blessing'—and a second head cranes out o' window. 'I'll give thee better sport than prayers and thou com'st to me,' I tells him. 'What then?' says Ned. 'Good skating yonder,' and I point to the Wele, a sheet of ice as it is this day. 'What, hast skates?' a' claps his hands. 'Not skates of Holland,' I confesses, 'we must do it in the old style on sheep-shanks—I have 'em under my tabard— and we'll find some stick or pole at the river-edge. So get a move on thee, for the wind's jolly nippy."

"You're sure you said that, Nick?"

"As good as. I tell thee what, a chap canna keep track o' *all* the slang a' hears in four hundred years. Ned says, 'How will I come? the outer room is full o' my people in a stupor, and I'm no bird to fly through the air.' 'Ay, but on a rope o' sheets,' thou piped. And 'twas done in a twinkling, and four of us were running iceward for our lives. And when we reached the Wele we let up such a shout as I wonder did not waken my Earl Rivers a mile away.

"We had the place to ourselves, for in those days the commoners didna herd on the river where it crossed the Bishop's privy fields, only little Marget in her furred hood crouched there, blowing her blue fingers, and then I knew why thou'dst hankered for the river-side.

"'Twas Ned and Nick and Geoff and Tom and Marget betwixt us soon enow, I warrant, and a merry hour we had cutting capers and teaching the Court boys how to skate on sheep's bones, clumsy contrivances to them accustomed to the fine new contraptions from the Netherlands, but the more rough-and-tumble the better the sport, and we was soon all heated with laughter. We had but the two pair o' shanks, and it was while thou and Geoffrey took a turn and skated off, Marget atween ye wi' a hand o' either for safety, that Ned's eye lights on my bishop's finery and he would be up to new games. 'Let's try 'em,' a' says, 'and thou take my purple—I'll be Bishop to thy Prince awhile.' So I helped him into all the gear, and donned his silk jerkin, though 'twas a sumptuary sin in itself for *me* to wear the purple—yet I vow neither felt a sinner, only a jolly boy; some things be hard to straighten, Tom. And a' strutted up and down and bade me do this and that i' the name o' the Church, and I defied him i' the name o' the Crown and a'vised him think o' Thomas Becket, and on that a' excommunicated me, and so I ran at him wi' his scabbard and gave him chase, and he fled like a hare, dropping mitre and crozier as he ran, but was sore cumbered wi' the robes—so at last I toppled upon him, and it was while we was rolling one over t'other that we heard thee scream.

"There was never a sight of thee when we looked; only in the dark distance we saw Geoffrey running like one out o' his wits, and Marget far-off standing in mid-ice, crying her loudest for us to come. Lord! how we took to our heels, Tom, I yelling thy name till I could yell no more for very hoarseness. I misremember how we came at last to the black water amid the broken ice where Marget shook and sobbed; but I was there afore Ned, who was still all bothered wi' those beastly robes. 'Where?' says I to Marget. 'Down there,' moans she; 'Geoffrey did it; a' tried to kiss me, and Tom hit him.' . . . Oh, Tom, 'twas a bad quarter-hour that next! I i' the water where I found thee and held on to thee wi' one arm, but could no more than keep thy head up ; and Ned full length on's stomach on the safe ice, gripping me lest I went under ; but each time a' crawled closer, the edge o' the ice gave, and we were but youngsters—we had na the means or the muscle to get thee out. It could ha' been done had Geoffrey Appsley stayed, but he went crazed wi' fear from the moment he pushed thee under, and we never saw him again. We didna notice Marget run, but she brought help to us anon. 'Twas Matt o' the Fenn she'd found abroad i' the fields, and he had snatched up the crozier as he sped, and that wi' his strength an' cunning soon settled matters. Oh, Tom, how blue and bad thou wast when we laid thee out. I thought thee dead then ; but we chafed thee and rubbed thee, our teeth all chattering vilely, and at last thou didst open thy eyes. . . ."

Nick paused.

The end of his story came with difficulty ; but this, I gathered, is what happened. Somehow I was smuggled into our quarters, and, with the help of a friendly servant, got to bed. Both Nick and I were in a bad way, but my ague was further advanced than his. Ned was caught, but never gave us away, and for his truancy was condemned to a sound beating. But Appsley being nowhere at hand to take it for him, the

Prince's governor demanded of Withun the name of one of his boys to serve in Geoffrey's stead. And Withun gave the name of the boy he loved the least, and one of the Prince's gentlemen was sent to fetch me.

Nick, who was in mortal scare for my life, and was battling with his chill until he might confess to Withun and make the best peace he could for us (for the prank was past hiding), asks—" What do ye want of Tom Thacker?"

"The loan of his body to salve the Prince's soul," laughs the courtier; and Nick looks grimly at the frightened choristers and says: "Well, I be ready," and goes in my name.

What followed is confusion. Nick, already in a fever, fainted under the ordeal, and came to himself on the bed he was never more to rise from in life. He recalls the end only through delirium—Hugh Withun's woe and fury at the bedside before he realised that the boy he loved was doomed; Nick's confession, and the old man's denunciation of the gross impiety of the prank; finally, the discovery of the loss of the owche from the holy paraphernalia, so hastily gathered together and smuggled into the Castle after the tragedy.

"Young sinful!" flares Withun in his favourite's ear: "I tell thee, till that sacred jewel be found thy ghost shall walk from Saint Nicholas to Holy Innocents. *Thou* to be a bishop, *thou* to preach a sermon to thy fellows—unfit! unfit! . . . ah, Nicholas Cope, Nick! . . ."

Nick never preached his sermon. When Holy Innocents dawned they were measuring him for his coffin.

V

I WIRED my expectant friends that I was ill, and settled down to three glad weeks with Nick. Whatever entertainment was going forward in Bridestow, there was no such sport as that afoot in Welchester, no such nights as I and my boy comrade passed in company. But you who read must be boys again, remember much and forget more, if you would understand. The glamour of adventure was upon us; we had an actual treasure to recover upon an ancient clue, and we made it the occasion of big deeds. Whether the owche had been dropped in Castle, mead, or river was past determining; and who knew that it lay where it was dropped? When we had haunted every cranny of the Castle ruins, from precipitous turrets, reached over the chasms of one-time stair-ways, to strange musty dungeons explored with candle-lamps, where we stirred up the dust and litter of God knows what experience of eld ; when we had dug the flats beneath the stars, and hunted their dim and endless trails in the pitchy dark ; when we had made the perilous voyage of the Wele on " skates of Holland " (O, joyous Nick! I bought two pair as soon as might be), had scoured its banks for miles on either hand, and dragged its danger-holes, bringing to light much curious matter, but never a hint of the jewelled owche ; a million chances of its ultimate fate opened new ways for us. We snatched at the thinnest pretext for wild trespasses which might have landed me in somewhat awkward places (it was Nick's secret woe that his ghostship rendered him immune from the delicious tremors of the transgressor) ; and his irresistible passion for door-bells resulted in more than one moment of difficult explanation for me, and unalloyed delight for the invisible truant.

One night when there was a bright moon we pitched our wickets on a deserted field, and Nick took his first instruction in the art of cricket—a mystery he had pined to solve " these hundred years."

IN THE MYDDES" 43

"To hear the choir-boys talk in summer," he said, "'tis somewhat after Handyn and Handoute, ha? but a sport to grow more crazed about than our old game. Lord! 'tis a hard matter to lie still i' the tomb and they chattering in whispers all about me! Didst ever see Jessop at the top o' his form, Tom? or Hobbs, or Alf Minn, or Ranji, or W. G.? What's a Test, Tom?"

I forget how we decided that cricket practice was to assist in the recovery of the owche, but I know that Nick developed symptoms of a googlie which would have turned Bosanquet green.

So night slipped after night, merry and magical and touched with an odd tenderness that did not lack its pangs as December drew to her close; and so Christ's Eve dawned and waned, and Nick and I lay under a hedge and watched the sunset fill the empty spaces of Welchester's ruins with magnificent pageantry. The golden west was like a call of clarions, and painted clouds rode past the hollow windows, a procession of brilliant images, scarlet that trampled the sky like horses' feet, purple that flowed in like a kingly mantle. And afar, that constant shouting of boys in the evening . . .

"Huzza! huzza!" Nick sprang to his feet

whirling his arms. " Welcome to the Prince! Welcome, Ned, welcome! Shout for him, Tom —huzza!"

"Huzza! huzza!" I joined my voice to his; and a small violet cloud, half fringed with gold, swam in the vacancy above the banquet-hall. . . .

That Christmas was a dark day, and shadows early filled the room in Margaret Venn's bakery where I sat awaiting the moment when my little Ghost would slip his tomb.

A party of singing children filed by the door, flooding the narrow alley with the strains of the Cherry-Tree Carol as they went; their voices passed into distance before they made an end. But one with a voice like the blackbird's pipe stayed under my window to give me the last words of the Christ-Child:—

> "O I shall be as dead, mother,
>   As the stones in the wall;
> O the stones in the streets, mother,
>   Shall mourn for me all.
>
> Upon Easter-day, mother,
>   My uprising shall be;
> O the sun and the moon, mother,
>   Shall both rise with me."

I ran down to reward the youngster, passing old Mrs. Venn in the shop.

"Going out, sir?" she smiled.

"That boy deserves a sixpence, mother; he has a voice like honey."

"What boy, sir?"

"Didn't you hear the carols, Mrs. Venn?"

"You'll hardly catch 'em now, my dear, they're long gone by."

I glanced at her, and opened the door on Nick lounging in its shadow.

"A glad Yule to thee, Marget Catton! A glad Yule, Tom."

"Can you still see the singers, sir?"

"Just the last of them. I say, what a wind! I'm leaving you in an awful draught, Mrs. Venn."

I shut myself outside with Nick, who was rubbing his brows rather soberly.

"Merry Christmas, Nick! You're out early."

"Ay. The Great Ones are sleeping. 'Tis my occasion."

"What would you like to do?"

"Shall we go carolling for our friends, Tom? There be many set about getting pennies from them that hear, but few enow to sing out o' love to the deaf. Let's tune up some of our favourites, Tom."

"I'm afraid I've forgotten a good deal."

"Thou'lt get it again from me. Let us sing the Levy-Dew for Marget. She liked that."

"But Marget isn't deaf, Nick."

"Ay, she be—century-deaf," said Nick with a catch in his throat. "So come now :—

"Here we bring new water
  From the well so clear,
For to worship God with,
  This Happy New Year.
Sing levy-dew, sing levy-dew,
  The water and the wine ;
The seven bright gold wires
  And the bugles they do shine.

"Sing reign of Fair Maid,
  With gold upon her toe,—
Open you the West Door.
  And let the Old Year go :
Sing reign of Fair Maid,
  With gold upon her chin—
Open you the East Door,
  And let the New Year in."

"Where now, Nick ? "

"To the graveyard," said he, and there we

turned ; and there, that Christmas afternoon, we lingered singing carols for the deaf.

For a newly-buried child Nick crooned the Virgin's Lullaby :—

> " This other night I saw a sight,
>   A mayd a cradle keep :
>   ' Lullay,' she sung, and said among,
>   ' Lie still, my child and sleep.' "

For an ancient lord he chose the Boar's Head Carol :—

> " The boares head in hands I bring,
>   With garlands gay and birds singing ;
>   I pray you all help me to sing.
>   *Qui estis in convivio.*"

Old words and airs came back to me in fragments as we crept among the graves in the falling darkness.

"Here be some of our fellows, here lies jolly Gregory," said Nick presently, as we found ourselves in the oldest part of the burying-ground. "Let's give 'em a rouser :—

> " The shepherd upon a hill he sat,
>   He had on him his tabard and his hat,

His tar-box, his pipe, and flagat;
And his name was called jolly jolly Wat.
For he was a good herd's-boy,
            Ut hoy!
For in his pipe he made so much joy."

There are ten verses in the Shepherd's Carol, and we sang them lustily from start to finish:—

"Now may I well both hope and sing,
For I have been at Christ's bearing;
Home to my fellows now will I fling;
Christ of heaven to His bliss us bring.
            Ut hoy!
For in his pipe he made so much joy."

"Gregory set store by yon," said Nick. He lay on his face and knocked the bitten grass. "Hillo, old boy, dost hear?" he called. "Tom," he sat up looking around with puzzled eyes, "what be they up to wi' the graves here? They be all digged about, and their stones down-turned."

"I think they've been shifting some of the coffins, Nick. I noticed it the day I came."

"Then 'tis a howling shame!" cried Nick. I heard his teeth chattering as he spoke. "Ay, 'tis! Why canna they leave old bones in peace?

IN THE MYDDES"

Hugh Withun lay yonder—see, even *his* monument uprooted too!" He ran forward and caressed the rotting slab that lay beside a pile of rubbish; broken earth and stones and splinters.

"Oh, Withun, where dost be? Can I not sing for thee as for the rest? Wilt never hear thy bad boy's voice again?—

> "'There is no rose of swych virtue
>   As is the rose that bare Jhesu.
>   *Alleluya!*'

"Which of all this dust be *thou*, Withun? laid open thus to the bitter air! . . . Tom, is that thee shivering?—

> "'For in this rose contained was
>   Heven and erth in litil space;
>   *Res miranda!*'

"Sing Tom, sing wi' me, for I canna keep my teeth steady. Try to like him, Tom, a' loved thy voice.

> "'By that rose we well may see,
>   There be one God in persons three;
>   *Pares forma!*

"——AND A PERLE

    The angeles sungen the shepherdes to
Gloria in excelsis Deo;
Gaudeamus!'

"What be this here?

  "' Leve we all this worldly mirth,'
                           [Look, Tom!]

    ' And follow we this joyful birth.
Transeamus!'

"Tom, what *is* it?"

VI

HE handed me a small and curious object: it appeared to be a box of iron, but a box that had no opening, being soldered about lid and hinge until one might have supposed it solid, but that something rattled within when it was shaken.

"Where did you find this, Nick?" I put my hand to my head, which was beginning to ache violently, and the wind cut through me with unendurable sharpness.

"Among yon rubble. Dost think thou canst

prise it open? My hands be so cold I canna put strength to it, yet my brain's like a stew full o' pepper. Do let's get at the innards, Tom."

"This needs tool-work, Nick. I'll have it opened to-morrow, and you shall see it in the evening."

"Ay, wilt thou be here?" said Nick, staring strangely.

"Yes, of course, old fellow. I say, get under my coat—this wind is freezing."

I felt his small body shaking and burning against mine.

"Art *very* angry wi' me?" he asked suddenly.

"I, Nick?"

"I know 'twas a folly, I know I shouldna ha' gone abroad in my gear, and the gloves, too. Thou didst warn me of that, but I was ever breaking rules. Withun, lift me up, the breath catches in my ribs."

"Nick. . . . Nick!"

"Ay, be thou not vexed wi' me, nor wi' Tom Thacker—see to Tom, wilt thou, Withun? he was never a tough one like me. I'll find my owche, old Withun, when I be better, I'll seek day and night till it be found, I will na rest till then. . . . Dost thou not say 'tis a sin o' my immortal soul until my owche be found? How shall I rest till then? . . ."

I prefer not to dwell upon the profound misery of the hours that followed. My annual illness had me in thrall, and Nick was in worse case than myself. He did not recognise me again. I do not remember how we parted, I only recall finding myself in the hands of old Mrs. Venn, and the darkest terror of that delirious night lay in the thought that the morrow might bring to me no Nick at all.

In the morning, to the woe of my kind nurse, I insisted on getting up. She must have found me a bad patient. I declined a doctor with vehemence; he would, I knew, forbid my outgoing. When Mrs. Venn saw me make for the door she wrung her hands.

"You'll catch your death!" she moaned.

"But I must go. I must find a smith."

I know she thought me out of my wits.

"What for, my dear?"

"I must get this open to-day." Nick's find was in my hand. I had made a promise, and its fulfilment was the last grace I could show him. It seemed to me as though I dared not go to meet him with that small casket still unopened.

"But it is Boxing-day, sir," she reminded me.

"Well, I must get hold of some one."

"Give it to me," she said soothingly. "I'll

see to it. Go sit by the fire now, do, my dear, and take your gruel."

In an hour she had returned, and laid the box beside me, its lid wrenched off. I did not examine the contents until I was alone. First a slip of parchment, scrawled with Latin in a crabbed and ancient hand—one sentence only,—

"*Lord, in the Day of Judgment when this sin shall come to light, have mercy on the souls of Hugh Withun and Nicholas Cope.*"

I knit my brows and tried to understand it. But the puzzle was beyond me. "This sin." What sin?

Returning to the casket, I shook out its sole remaining contents: an antique brooch of beaten gold, set with four dulled gems and a pearl in the middle.

VII

NOTHING now would have kept me from seeking Nick this day, and I prayed from my soul for a glimpse of him—an instant's respite only in which to restore to him the lost treasure that would bring him joy and peace.

When dusk came I watched my opportunity, eluded my nurse, and slipped out, muffled in my warmest things. In the pocket of my greatcoat lay the thrice-precious jewel.

I looked for Nick first about the Cathedral grounds, but he was not there. Then I turned in the direction of the Castle, and among the ruins I found him—stretched out on the floor of the room where, he had told me, we boys had been wont to sleep. He was flushed and breathing heavily, and seemed half-conscious only; but my step aroused him, and he welcomed me with eyes too bright.

"Where hast been so long?" he said.

"Nick, I've news for you, good news!"

"Ay, but let me speak. Oh, I have forgot my sermon, and Holy Innocents is hard upon us. When is it? To-morrow! Nay, next day. Bring me my sermon to con, I shall make hash of it else."

"Never mind your sermon, dear old chap. Listen——"

"Ay, let sermon go. I shallna speak it, I reckon. Now tell me, Withun"—(the name was an arrow in my heart)—"tell me *truly*, if I die afore my owche be found, must my spirit walk from Saint Nicholas to Childermas—must it, Withun?"

"IN THE MYDDES"

"Yes, but, Nicholas——"

"Withun! Withun!" Two feverish little hands gripped me. "Let me not die afore my term be out! let me not, Withun. I do na want to be buried among the bishops; I want to lie wi' my mates. What will I do the year-long in that solemn place, that house o' stone where the sun so rarely comes? Lonely I'll lie there, and full o' longing. I be a boy, I be no bishop—I want the earth and the air, and the moon and the sun, and the sound o' boys' feet trampling in the grass, and the call o' boys' voices in the playing-fields, and the hearts o' my fellows beating wi' mine under the living sod. Oh, Withun, shall I die afore my term be sped? Lift me a little—the breath hurts still— I want to see thy eyes to tell me truly . . . I canna see them, they be too wet. . . . Ay, well. So I must lie i' the Church wi' the old ones and the great ones, I that be young and small; but, ha, ha! Withun! I shall a little cheat 'em! I shall escape 'em once in a twelvemonth, eh? I shall get my Holy-day come each December, eh? I have thy word for that—my three good weeks to seek the owche I lost; oh, never, never, never be it found! . . .

"What was thy news?"

"My news, old fellow?"

"Ay, thy good news, Withun."

"Why . . . that Tom Thacker's better, Nick, and sends his love."

"Give him mine, Withun. Look to him kindly, Withun. Oh, Withun, lift me up . . ."

But there was nothing to lift. The ghost of Nicholas Cope slipped through my arms.

VIII

Repassing the Cathedral, before I turned the angle of the East Wall I heard an anvil clinking in the night. "Catton's at some work," I thought. My hand thrust into my pocket closed on the fragments of the iron box whose contents Withun had carried to his grave. "To-morrow I will get this re-soldered." I came round the corner where Catton's forge once stood.

The cold wall only met me, the ring of the hammer fell silent . . . but was it imagination that an old spare figure, with a face like puckered parchment, slid past me out of the shadows hugging a secret object to its breast? . . . I turned my head and there was nothing.

"God rest your soul, Hugh Withun," I said,

IN THE MYDDES"

"and let us be friends at last; for I too have found our boy's lost owche, and taken the guilt of its loss on my own shoulders for his dear sake."

That night in my room I added three words to the Latin script upon the parchment, and the tiny casket, which was soldered in my presence on the morrow, contained, besides the jewel, a plea for mercy on the souls of Hugh Withun, Nicholas Cope, and Thomas Thacker.

IX

On the morning of the 28th I attended service in the Cathedral. It was against my nurse's wish, but my chill was abating, and this was to be my valediction to Welchester. Nothing now detained me, and I meant to join my friends in Bridestow with as little delay as possible.

As I entered the doors I passed my old verger, and a moment later heard him whisper to one behind me—

"Your gentleman still looks very bad."

"He's better than he was, Mr. Withers," murmured a voice I knew, and glancing back I saw that Margaret Venn was following in my wake. She looked a scared apology, but I smiled and waited for her, and we took our seats together.

I could not fix my thoughts on the service. Concentration is difficult in certain periods of convalescence. Most of the time I sat with my hands over my eyes, thinking of Nick lying not far away, and wondering whether he found the sermon dull. The text, as being appropriate I suppose to the day, was " Suffer little children. . . . " I hardly heard the words, but the voice of the preacher was of a wonderful sweetness.

. . . . .

A soft hand touched my knee. I uncovered my eyes. Beside me sat a little girl, a charming child, rosy and smiling. I had not observed her before. Nor had I observed that the entire congregation was one of children, their eyes, alert and friendly beyond the wont of youngsters in church, all fixed upon the pulpit. No, there was one man among the flock, a lean old fellow, in a black robe, sitting in a far corner ; and his eyes also burned upon the preacher. The children were dressed in a fashion familiar to me ; I glanced down at my own long hose. . . .

"*Tom!*"
"*Hello, Marget!*"
"*Doesna he look splendid!*"

Then I, too, turned to the pulpit, and there saw Nicholas Cope in all his bravery. He grinned across at me, and had ado, I knew, not to wave his hand.

". . . and lastly," said Nicholas Cope, " I tell ye this. Christ has a liking for fun and good sport and a laughing heart, A'll damn no boy for pure mischief, so it *was* pure mischief—for, fellows, mischief can be crooked too ; and we all know, better than them that leathers us after the act, whether ours was the crooked sort or no. And, another thing, a chap must learn to take his own leatherings—ay, though he be a prince he must !—and to bear 'em wi' a good grace and not whimper, for 'twas up to him if a' chose to swallow the jam afore a' gulped down the powder, and don't ye forget it. It's cheek o' me to be up here talking morality at ye when ye all know me the worst truant o' the pack : I never could keep my mind o' my book when window was open and earth called . . . but God made the earth, and man only made the lesson, an' I don't believe He's angry wi' a chap for loving His work the better o' the two—He shouldna ha' made boys and ice to be in one season if He hadna wanted 'em to come together. May He forgive me my sins ; I've had a jolly good time, and I canna think He grudged me. For Christ's Self was one time a child like us, and that's why A' keeps a smile for our mirth so well as a tear for our sorrow.

"Let us now sing the Carol o' the Cherry-Tree to the glory of the Virgin and her Child—up wi' ye all, and lustily :—

> "'Joseph was an old man
> And an old man was he.'"

Voices of children, a bright wave of them, flooded the Cathedral to the roof. But something checked my throat, and Nick I could scarcely see for a swimming in my eyes. I only knew that he was looking fixedly upon me through all the singing, and that before the final verse he was descending from the pulpit and coming my way. Beside my seat he paused, and his voice rang in my ear like a bell heard in a mist :—

> "O I shall be as dead, Tom,
>   As the stones in the wall ;
> O the stones in the streets, Tom,
>   Shall mourn for me all.

"Upon Saint Nicholas next, Tom,
   My uprising shall be,
O the sun and the moon and thou,
   Tom Thacker,
Shall all rise with me. . . ."

. . . . .

"Are you not coming?—d⸢ you feel so bad, my dear?"

The congregation was almost dispersed. Margaret Venn and I alone kept our seats.

"In a few minutes, mother. No, I'm as right as rain—really. Trot home now; I'll be there soon to get my box strapped."

She left me; and I stepped along the empty grandeur of that place, once to touch in farewell the hand of Nicholas Cope, where he lay among the noble tombs of four of Mother Church's brightest gems, a pearl in their midst.

X

On my friend's estate in Bridestow there is a well reported to be bottomless. Soon after my arrival I demanded an introduction to it, and my hostess, full of welcome and commiseration, led the way.

"Too bad, you missed the best of the fun," she chattered. "You don't look very grand even now—I hope you didn't come on to us too soon—however, we'll nurse you round as fit as a fiddle for New Year and Twelfth Night. And next year you must be sure and be here for Christmas."

"I'm afraid you mustn't count on me."

"Oh, come now!" She shook her head laughingly. "A prior engagement, I suppose?"

"Yes, a prior engagement."

"So likely, isn't it! Here's the well. You wouldn't believe how long it is before one hears the splash. Let's find a stone or something."

"This will do," I drew my hand from my pocket.

"What is it? (There! have you dropped it?) Nothing that matters, I hope. It's past recovery now till Judgment Day. Listen!"

Faint and far I heard the splash.

"THE SHEPHEARD'S GYRLOND"

I

SHEPHEARDS ! anie tyme I see
Blossome dauncing on a tree,
  I doe thynke upon hir.
When I see a flying bird
Sinking suddenlie unheard
To the oceans creamie curd,
  Then I thynke upon hir.

When a shining lawne I view
Speckled with the morning dew,
  I doe thynke upon hir.
When I see a moonie cloude
Thatte too nigh the Witch hath straied
Charm-bound in a siluer shroude,
  Then too thynke I on hir.

When I smell th' enchaunted muske
Of awak'ning floweres at duske
  I doe thynke upon hir.
Or when litil riuers leape
Tinkling downe an emerauld steepe
Where th' enamelled florets peepe,
  Then I thynke upon hir.

66 "THE SHEPHEARD'S GYRLOND"

Whenas the skyes are sapphire wells
Lit with sunnie miracles,
  I doe thynke upon hir.
Anie tyme when starr-beames shake
Lances thatte with snowe-light flake
Willowes dreaming by a lake,
  Thynke I much upon hir.
O at manie plesaunt springs
Doe my fancies fledge theyr wings !
I nere looke on prettie things
  But I doe thynke upon hir.

Nathaniel Downes, variously appearing as Nat Douns, Nathaniell Dones, Master N. Doones—but, in any guise, the " Natty " of George Peele's sometime and most unreliable affections—come forth from the retirement where even our modern anthologist has left you to languish ! For you are worthy, at least of this momentary word, this fleeting notice ; and if, after your three centuries of rest, they fail to endue you with that life which certain dead rhymesters, no better than yourself, continue to enjoy, then return once more and for ever to your dreams beneath the kindly Sussex sod that shelters your dust.

It is really something remarkable that Nat has so completely dropped out of the recognised

"THE SHEPHEARD'S GYRLOND" 67

circle of the Elizabethans ; for that he was a graceful, though not a great, poet, is plain after a perusal of his pamphlet of verse, assembled under the title standing at the head of this paper. If we except his entertaining " Diurnall," from which autobiographical common-book we draw our main knowledge of him (it was not, however, published until the Restoration ; by some grand or great-grand-child, one supposes, and copies are very hard to come by), " The Shepheard's Gyrlond " is his only preserved work. It was printed during his lifetime ("By E. F. for Thomas Fowle, and are to be solde at the signe of the Angell in Paules Churchyard, 1594") ; and if it was quicklier forgotten than the lyrics of his contemporaries, this may well be due to the fact that he was not a dramatist as well as a poet. Some slight and beautiful songs still live for us which might have been eternally lost but that their authors' names are shored up by monuments of stage-stuff not now actable, and read only by the student whose business it is to know the values of the dramatic renaissance at the close of the sixteenth century. Had good Tom Heywood, for instance, never produced a certain bulk of not too-inspirational plays, would not his one golden lyric have slipped for ever through the crannies of men's memories ? But there it is, a charming cameo preserved to the world by a dull and massive frame, simply because Tom dwelt—as Nat did not—a humble muse on that Parnassus of Drama whose Phœbus-Apollo was William Shakespeare. And so our anthologist seldom omits " Pack, clouds, away " from his Elizabethan bouquet ; to add one whiff to whose fragrance he is now commended to a closer acquaintance with " The Shepheard's Gyrlond." (My friend, the Anthologist—my friend, Master Nathaniel Downes!)

And while the admitted purpose of the present chronicler is to reintroduce the best of this pretty collection to a forgetful public, it may be found that Nat's own life-story, so artlessly set down in his " Diurnall," has an engaging aspect of its own. Incurably whimsical, even at his most wistful he cannot conceal the dimple round the corner, nor do his pair of tear-drops succeed in dimming a twinkling optic.

Let us get to facts.

Nathaniel Downes, on his specific statement, was Kentish born, although the Sussex he died in has claimed him. He is negligent of his dates, but we may fix his birth between 1569-73. In his early childhood his family removed over the borderland of its native shire into Sussex. The events of his life call for small comment till

"THE SHEPHEARD'S GYRLOND"

he runs away to London, the Mecca of the Elizabethan poet; a pilgrimage Nat was bound to make at some period in his existence, for the poet sang in his veins, and was, it may be added, very little appreciated by his kin. He seems to have been apprenticed to a blacksmith, one Jno. Wynne, who reappeared later to some purpose in Nat's history. Nat tells us :—

"The iron wold grow cold on the anuill whiles I didd string my rhymes. Then my master did beat mee."

Was it after one such basting that Nat, a lad of eighteen or twenty, took his beloved gittern and turned his face Londonward "withouten a grote in mye pouch"?

He sang his way, and as frequently starved his way, to the city; and now we see him arriving sorefoot at the Three Pigeons, by Lambeth Stairs, on a morning when merry George Peele was playing host there to a party of friends.

"I heard loud talk and laughter within," Nat tells us, "and looking through the window spied a jolly company at dinner. Whereat my empty belly ached towfold and my parched tongue took a double flame."

Some one flung a scrap to a hound, and the sight seems to have driven the boy to desperation.

For he pokes his head through the casement and cries :

"I would I also went on four feet, my master! I am leaner than thy dog."

We can imagine the astonishment of the roysterers. It was Peele, of course, who waved the hand of welcome, saying :

"Art lean enough to creep through the casement and beg, dog?"

Nat worms his way in (no easy task with certain windows of the period, so his entrance is, in some sort, his argument), and the company begins to make sport with him.

He is asked, "What wilt thou?"

"A full flagon," says Nat.

"Hast aught to barter therefor?"

"Ay," says Nat, "a dusty throat."

"A short bargain, boy."

"No," says Nat, "'tis the length of this road to Sussex coast."

"Why, why, why!" cries George, "then Thames' self will scarce fill it."

"Yet this puddle had served," says Nat, and looks at the floor, running spilled liquor.

"I think thou'st some wit," observes George.

"I do know I've much thirst," responds Nat, and by this he is growing really faint; but don't expect heart in such company. They are not

"THE SHEPHEARD'S GYRLOND"

yet done with him. Let the lout stand up to them till he drop; then, doubtless, they will pick him up again.

Some one says, "I see thou hast a very pretty gittern. Your true, raging, not to-be-denied thirst had sold it long before ye were over Sussex border."

Poor Natty!

"'Gentles,' I saies, 'I mought as soone roaste and dine off the hart in my bodie to preserue myselfe from staruing. If I part with my gitterne I part with my trade.'"

George asks, "What is thy trade?"

"I sing for a living," says Nat.

"What songs dost thou sing?" asks George.

"Mine own songs," says Nat.

George looks Nat up and down at this, peers in his pinched and smiling face, observes his rags and his grime and his country slouch, and then says very gravely, but winking one eye at his friends:

"Praise the fair day on which I discover mine own brother! Brother, sing us a song."

And Nat, for all his parched throat, very readily sings.

The "Diurnall" does not quote his song. It may have been a fugitive verse, made one day and forgotten the next, when it had won him a bed or a supper. But if it appears among those preserved in the " Gyrlond," we can well imagine it to be the pretty twelve-line lyric that runs—

> O haue ye euer seene a woode
>   Wher in the yeares greene infancie
> Yong violets are thicklie strewd,
>   A coole contentment to the eie?
>
> Or haue ye euer hird a nest
>   Of hidden byrdès that when daie
> Sleepes on the golden-pillow'd West
>   Doe sing the laste of lyghte awaie?
>
> Soe tender and so yong to see
>   Is she my bosome onely loues,
> And in such singing puritie
>   Among my thoghts and praiers sche moues.

Whether it was this song or another, we gather that the audience was both surprised and delighted; and, indeed, smooth rhythm and sound rhyming, eked out with less imagination than we know Nat capable of, would alone have been bound to achieve their effect in a company that was looking for something very different. Generosity succeeded to banter; the singer had obliterated the rustic. George loudly proclaims the young man's gittern to be the third and least part of his stock-in-trade; his voice is its master, and his fancy betters his voice. What is the rhymester's name? Nat supplies it.

"Thy lady's name, too," is next demanded, "for so sweet an one is worthy a toast."

And now—alack and alack, and yet again alack!—our Nat commits himself to the fatal words. He says:

"Elizabeth Wynne," and unconsciously sets the seal upon his destiny.

The impulse that made him utter the lie is one of the things for which we find him likeable.

For we have his word that up to this time Natty's affections had never been seriously engaged. He had no lady. His songs of love were composed to that idealised figment we all cherish in the abstract, and pop straightway into the first concrete body that attracts us, irrespective of the fitness of the idol to its shrine. Hence too many tragedies. But Nat not yet having encountered the shrine to contain his idol, Peele's demand embarrassed him. The truth was the last thing to be uttered in the circumstances.

"I saw," he frankly confesses, "my gentlemen expectant of a name, and I was loth to disoblige them. Moreover, I had to make capital of their interest in me, and durst not let it wane for lack of a lady. So casting about in my mind I named the last wench of my native place that ever, poor soul, was like to have a lover. There was few there went a-begging for kissings, mine own mouth is testimony thereto, but her age and her defects denied her other maid's glories, and I thinks it will do sad Mistress Wynne no hurt to be loved a little in my songs."

Kind-hearted Nat! in answer to that query he might have elected the rosiest lip in Sussex, or the brightest eye of his dreams; and instead he makes choice of his master's sallow sister, and breathes out her name as though it crowned the very queen of loveliness:

"Elizabeth Wynne!"

The lady is acclaimed by the company.

"Here's to Bess Wynne," says George ("verie aptlie"), "and may Nat win Bess!"

A joke that some three centuries leave stale. But we are to-day not without our comedians at whose quips it is conceivable another hundred years will shrug.

Nat thanks the company for this double toasting of himself and his sweetheart, "but," he adds, "ye mought toaste me my sire and my dam and mye brethren and sistren to boote,

"THE SHEPHEARD'S GYRLOND" 75

and al this drynking wold nott make my throte enie the less drye. I praie you yowre names, gentles, and I will toaste ye seuerallie."

Amid laughter he is given to drink, and it "sett my harte afyre, thogh my stommicke was still a bagge of wind."

Nothing now contents George Peele but he will have Natty to London to make a poet of him.

"He will fatten thee, he will fatten thee, Master Downes," cries one, jerking his head at the window.

But George, pulling a wry face, "Nay, never fear it, Natty. We poets go lean to the worms. I that ha' been at the trade a year to thy every month could still follow where thou leddest."

He pushes the somewhat bewildered Nat to the window and, as though to prove his point, bundles him out, leaping fantastically after to the mirthful applause of the room. Neither Nat nor the company is quite aware of what is happening, but George knows very well. Instead of re-entering the tavern with his new friend, he hurries him to the waterside where "a paire of oares," hired by one of his guests, is in waiting.

"To London swiftly," says George, pulling Nat with him; "this matter cannot wait.

Master Lovatt will have thee return for him by supper."

George accomplished these things with an air. The " paire of oares " obeyed unquestioningly, and the guests were left in the " Ordinarie" to settle their host's account. It is Nat's first experience of George Peele's little way.

Well! at last we have Nat treading London City, but we will not ask him for his immediate impressions ; because—

"By this my head did something buzz." The natural effect of strong drink on an empty stomach. Peele notes it.

"What, my ruddy Nat!" says he ("but wheather in iest of my white cheakes or my redd mop I knowe not "), " what's amiss ? "

Nat, between rueful and roguish, admits to having tasted nothing since yesternoon. George falls a-thinking. Penniless as usual, he is to sup at a tavern on the invitation of a friend ; and the incident now related in the " Diurnall" is worth quoting, because it is plainly the source of one of that prolific family of " merry jests " whereof loose report had made George so indiscriminate a parent. Thanks to Nat's evidence, this particular trick of his begetting may henceforth stand legitimatised among many bastards. Strolling the streets, an arm about Nat's shoulder,

"THE SHEPHEARD'S GYRLOND" 77

George bends his mind to the problem of winning the boy a supper. He regrets not having fed his young friend in Lambeth, at the expense of Master Lovatt or another. As it is—

"I cannot bid thee to sup with me in Friday Street, Natty; am but a guest myself. And to speak plain thy rags be not overnice for a gentleman's board. But we may devise something."

Briefly, the "something" is devised, Natty instructed, and George in due course repairs to the tavern, where he is warmly welcomed by a company more reputable than that frequenting the Lambeth ordinary. We must not forget that George was a man of gentle birth, fine education, and exquisite talents; advantages not incompatible with the slack sense of morals which distinguished him even in an age that had no finicking palate for morality. The meal is in full swing, Natty biding his time without; and so soon as the meat is carried in, in too swaggers Master Downes, half-insolence, half-servility, and plants himself before Peele at the upper end of the table. George gives vent to an exclamation, and the company may plainly perceive that he is acquainted with this fellow; who is, then, no purely unauthorised interloper.

"How now, you ******** rogue!" cries George. "What make you here?"

"Sir," answers Natty, pregnant with meaningless meanings, " I am from the party you wot of."

The interruption now becomes explicable to the company. George's habits are well known here. The anonymous " party " may be either a creditor or a mistress.

"What, what!" says George. "Will you still be troublesome? Will you not be warned?"

"Sir, hear my errand," says Nat (and it had been like George to leave him to tell it! but he can keep faith occasionally). He will hear nothing, and screams at Natty like a shrew, since his high pipe permits him not to roar like a lion.

"Will you be talking, do you prate, slave?" cries he, and at that, writes Nat, " Geo. catched up a pye and flung it at my head."

Nat grabs at it, as to save himself, saying, "You use me ill, sir."

"Do I so, do I so?" ramps George, and a " loafe " follows the " pye." This has all passed swiftly, and George is in such a heat of rage that the company rises to allay him. Time enough; for he has whipped out his dagger, fury-possessed. In those days tragedies happened lightning-wise; two or three lay hands on him, remonstrating with, soothing him; and one, taking Nat by the shoulders, whispers to him to be gone

"THE SHEPHEARD'S GYRLOND" 79

for his life's sake. He probably imagines that he is doing George a good turn in thus getting rid of the importunate fellow ; and in a manner he is, for this is the natural consummation of the "jest." Natty's heels are out at door and round corner in a flash, and he sups contentedly on his loaf and his pie without, while George permits himself to be pacified within.

The two meet anon, and George takes Nat home to sleep at his house " on the Banckside." Nat is commended for his playing of the part, and is promised others as profitable.

"Thou'st shown," says George, "such aptness to filch thy dinner from the board that thou shalt henceforth tread the boards for thy dinner." Our earliest intimation of Nat the actor.

Nat the poet has perhaps been kept too long a-waiting. We come to him now. At George's home he sees George's daughter Anisia, "a litil handsom damsell, scarce aboue fifteene somers as I thinck." This is his first mention of lovely Annys Peele. To Mrs. Peele there is no reference whatever ; and as little is heard of her in George's own life (save that he married a lady's fortune and squandered it), we may take it that she was by this time dead. Dates play will-o'-the-wisp with us here. George's own birth-year is in doubt ; but Annys, as we now meet her, seems to relegate him to the very early fifties, in defiance of Malone's 1558—which, if correct, would make George a member of Pembroke College (then Broadgates Hall) at the age of six! The young scholar must have been just in his teens when his name appeared in the University Matriculation book of 1564, and was probably twenty when elected a student of Christ Church in 1573; and he was evidently married and Annys born before he received his degree of M.A. in 1579. As she was "scarce aboue fifteene somers" when the "Diurnall" mentions her, we may approximate it that Nat came to London between 1591-93. This is as near as conjecture will bring us. The "Gyrlond" is dated 1594; and if George Peele, a year or so before this, had a daughter of fifteen summers, he must (unless we dispute Malone) have fathered her somewhat precociously at nineteen. Natty's evidence, then, is all in favour of those historians who believe George to have been born in 1552 or 1553. As to Nat himself, the "Gyrlond's" date allows for the lapse of anything from eighteen months to three years between his arrival in and his departure from London. It may indeed have been printed after Nat's marriage and retirement; but when the facts are considered, this seems unlikely.

"THE SHEPHEARD'S GYRLOND" 81

How soon did Nat begin to warm to Annys? Sooner, I dare swear, than the "Diurnall" confesses or than he himself was conscious of. She must have been easy to love, the naughty witch. And Natty early mentions a frequenter of the Peele household—T. (Thomas?) Waulshell or Walsell—a sober lover of hers, nigh thirty, and says Nat with the young poet's scorn, "in trade a mercer, a vender of cloaths by the measure, a' had no traffic in measureless dreams."

And perhaps no worse a fellow for that, Master Nat!

But let us consider the poet in the making. If the verses of the "Gyrlond" appear in chronological order, we may take it that the earliest are not addressed to Annys. Ostensibly they are all dedicated to Elizabeth Wynne; but of course she inspired none of them, and served but as the figurehead Natty must sing to. Cast suddenly among a world of dazzling minds and unimagined romance, his muse cannot escape the imitative. Most young creators follow models to begin with. So, from fashion, Nat's mistress becomes an "unkynde" one, which gives him scope for pretty plaints; and, from fashion too, he catches the trick of classical allusion, as witnesseth one of the earliest songs—

"THE SHEPHEARD'S GYRLOND"

On a greenswarde wher I chaunced
Maydens and theyr shepheards daunced.
One, the fayrest of the bande,
Ran to take me by the hande.
Charming Childe (I sayd) acquitt me!
Chearful motions ill doe fit me.
How toe daunce can I haue minde
While my loue lookes still unkynde?

In a rosie gardin I
Did a singing partie spye.
One, the sueetest dulcimer,
Bade me joyn my voice with hir.
Bird of June (I sayd) forego me!
Tunefull straines no moe doe know me,
And to sing I haue no minde
While my loue lookes still unkynde.

Al among a woody glade
Venus selfe my footsteps staied,
Who in pitie of my woes
Offer'd me hyr mouths twin rose.
Goddesse! (sayd I) hauing slaine me
How to kiss shalt thou constraine me?
For Loues owne lips I haue no minde
Until my true loues lips prooue kynde!

Rather quaintly in this song occurs the

"THE SHEPHEARD'S GYRLOND"

" dulcimer " of the second verse, a reference to the sweet instrumentalist by the title of her sweetly named instrument. But we can see that the poet has as yet suffered no real pang—it is the delicate assumption of pain only. The song to Sleep, too, is little more than an exercise in the graceful imagery of the period, with an experimental use of the Alexandrine of the Spenserian stanza in a verse which otherwise departs from the Spenserian form—

> Come downe to dwelle againe uponne myne eies,
>   O golden sleepe !
>   Thou that dost steepe
> Our soberst thoghts in rainebowe-colour'd dyes
> And patterne them with threades of cunning phantasies.
>
> Thou blossome of the darkling wombe of nyghte,
>   Thou magicke rose
>   Dost droune our woes
> With constant visions of perfumèd light
> Pour'd from thy streaming hart of visions most fayre and bright.

"THE SHEPHEARD'S GYRLOND"

Uponne thy pearle and siluer thrones
of dreame
    Men are croun'd kings
    And rise on wings
Of yvorie and amber toe the
gleame
Of starres that in daies whelming glare
alle lost doe seeme.

Euen soe the ymage of my cold loue
waites
    Within thy halls,
    And when nighte falls
With her owne handes undoes the
christall gates,
Transform'd by thee to loue thatte
which sche now most hates.

One other may be quoted here, one of the freshest and least " borrowed " in its effect, as an example of how Nat is beginning to think for himself. There is a considerable limbering of his style in the last verse, which reflects rather happily his own natural capacity to sigh and smile simultaneously. The " Save Mary " in the second verse is also significant, smacking Catholic in a particularly Protestant age. Yet it may mean less than it appears to : poets are conscienceless, and "Mary" was just the foot needful in that place.

> Vnderneath my sueet hart's bowre
>   I tried to tune my oaten reed,
>   But O! it wold not serue my need,
>   It was al musicke run to seed
> Manie a somer past its flowre.
>
> Vnderneath my sueet harts bowr
>   Then I tryde to sing a staue,
>   But O! it was a brokenne waue
>   Of sound from musickes ocean. (Saue
> Mary she bee not home this hour!)
>
> She did from her bowre-windowe looke—
>   "O Shepheard, what a sorrie song!"
>   "Ay was it, ladie!" Laught she long.
>   With laughter left I hir—so strong
> I thynke she heard not how it shooke.

All this would considerably have astonished Mistress Wynne! Certainly she had never shown Nat any more encouragement than the Shepheardess his "Gyrlond" sighs for, and thus far she fitted the part. She was in any case accepted by Nat's London acquaintance as his own dear, cruel-hearted love, and he could not very well undeceive them. But . . .

But does not the last-quoted song begin to smack of personal experience? in the place of pictured cruelty and imagined distress, have we not here an actual laugh and a positive sigh? does it not savour less of impalpable Elizabeth Wynne, than of warm-blooded, mocking, mischievous Annys Peele?

Turning the pages of the "Gyrlond" and the "Diurnall" side by side, we find that at this point both begin to throb a little.

II

Doe not soe froune upon me, sueete com-
plainder !
　Your case is lesse then myne for swifte
　reliefe,
Your grievance not soe large but some
remaynder
　Of aunger mooues there—myne is onely
　greife.

Rage hath lifes heate in it, despayre deaths
chilling !
　Lett each of th' others woe be pityfulle—
That you unwilling beare two hartes,
unwilling
　That I no moe beare anie hart at alle.

Had Annys been born as little as sixty years
later, we should have no more discussions as
to the identity of the First Actress. Mistress
Hughes, Mistress Saunderson, and the rest of
'em, would have curtsied in the van of Anisia
Peele. Report has it that at the age of ten she

was as good an actress as George an actor, whose delight it was to instruct her how to abet his sharper's tricks. Whether this is true or not, we know that she had a lively disposition and was inured to a life of doubtful shifts, the seamy side of which, poor child, she was probably, through custom, incapable of judging. George seesawed between plenty and penury, and Annys swung on his knee and adored him. She was accustomed to have her finger in his pie, and so, of course, she must have it in his young pupil's. She, as well as George, will undertake Nat's education; if *he* will make Master Downes a poet, *she* will add the crowning grace of making Master Downes a lover.

At first in the "Diurnall" it is "Mistris Peele," then "Mistris Anisia," finally (and with very little delay about the matter), plain "Annys."

To her he brings his poems, half-completed. This she praises, that she will none of.

"Thy father likes it very well, Mistress Anisia."

"His daughter likes it very ill, Master Downes."

"He commends the workmanship of it."

"She condemns the heart in it."

"What's amiss with the heart?"

"Why, it hath none! Oh, the manner will

serve, Master Downes, but the matter, Lord! would tingle no maid's blood."

Be sure that if she will have it altered, altered it is.

To her he brings his parts, half-learnt—little parts all, for no man is an Alleyn or a Tarleton to begin with, yet still hard for Nat to master. "Study and I were ever cold friends," he tells us, "and words would slip through my mind like water through a man's fingers." But Annys was helpful, she drummed his lines into his noddle, and generally taught him how to utter them, acting them before his eyes with a captivating variety of mood. She likes his humour well enough, but scoffs at his sentiment.

"Thou'rt but a lack-lustre lover, Master Nat! Shine a little, warm a little, young sir! imagine thyself addressing thy shepheardess, and she kind for the nonce."

Small wonder if Annys is the one person shrewd enough to suspect the genuineness of the boy's ardour for Elizabeth Wynne—even before he gave her personal cause to change suspicion into certainty.

Then Nat describes the scene when, on a sunny day, they sat together on the stone bench in her "litil inclosd herb-gardin." He writes vividly enough for us to fill in the details of the picture and the colour of their emotions. The sun is coining silver on the wave of the Thames, bees are busy among the scented borders, and Nat and Annys begin to be aware of one another.

She twits him on the slow progress which, to judge by his verse, he makes with his "Shepheardess."

"You sigh overmuch," she declares, "and that, believe it, is the weakest weapon in a man's armoury. You should sigh less and kiss more."

Nat glances sidelong. "But if I have not her leave to kiss?"

"Then kiss her without. I will not believe you never kissed her."

Nat "feigns coy" and looks "scarified." "Not her nor any!"

"Nor been kist neither?" mocks she.

Nat edges from her shyly. "Maids kiss not first. Indeed I never knew the taste of kissing."

"There's for you, then, my simple lover!" says she, and plumps a kiss full on his mouth that she "mought laugh to see me putt out of countenance therby." As though the fisherman were disconcerted by that he has angled for! Not at all out of countenance, Nat catches his instructress to his breast and twice smacks her lips right lustily. She stares a moment and then falls a-laughing.

"THE SHEPHEARD'S GYRLOND"

"O, Nat !" she cries, " y'are a naughty rogue, and I am such another !"

At that " I didd make to buss her a iiid tyme but shee will not, and runs all mirth shakenne out of my armes so swifte I cannot ouertake her."

From which hour she falls to plaguing Nat, and he to loving in good earnest.

Soon after this, it may be, the " Gyrlond " flowers with the following couplets—

> A rogue is in hir dimpled cheake, an angell in her eie,
> The rogue doth make a mocke of mee, the angell passes by.
>
> Hir left hande is a crueltie, hir ryghte hande a caresse,
> Shee laies hir left hande on my hart that cries hir tendernesse.
>
> Hir bosome is an ingelnooke, hir tresses are a snare,
> And I am netted comfortlesse among hir windie haire.
>
> Hir spirit is a charitie, hir lips a house of scorne,
> And I haue dwelt upon hir lips synce euer I was borne.

The song smacks more of merry Annys Peele than of mysterious Elizabeth Wynne; we cannot doubt whose spirit lurks within it; which makes the final line doubly instructive. Foxy Nat pulls himself up with a jerk, puts Annys off the scent with a subtle touch. Not so swiftly will he own himself traitor to his Shepheardess, "upon whose lips," sings he, " I have dwelt *since ever I was born*." This fits Bess Wynne, his elder; had he sung of Annys, must he not have written, "I have dwelt upon her lips since ever *she* was born"?

Well, even he could hardly have proclaimed as much after knowing Annys a handful of months—and he could not destroy a pretty sentiment in the couplet—and he could not so barefacedly renounce an old love for a new—and ah! for all this, we know very well that the rogue he sang was Annys. In a succeeding poem we detect him in subterfuge again. Mistress Peele was dark, Mistress Wynne "straw-coloured"; but this song too is Anisia's, despite the reference to golden locks. Transparent Nat! the locks of your "pretty may" were not golden by nature, they were the hue of night, dye you them never so deep in the dawn.

"THE SHEPHEARD'S GYRLOND"

Alle in a meadow fayre at the break of day
I did see my prettie loue with siluer dazies play.
  Happie (sayd I) happie dazies
  That soe well can win hir prayses
Who not prayses Loue himselfe ne will not looke hys way!

Downe from her golden head alle hir haire she shooke
Stouping lowe to drynk awhyle at a running brooke.
  Happie waters that doe dayre
  Lapp her mouth and tresses fayre
Who at Loues owne rosie mouth nere hir plesure tooke.

Prettie may, froward may! yourselfe doe ply the suit!
I tax not you as you tax me, O wherfor will ye do't?
  'Tis your very fayre doth grieve ye,
  Bee unlovelie and I'll leave ye—
Ye shold nott flowre so in my hart if ye will beare no fruit!

"THE SHEPHEARD'S GYRLOND"

After this we discover no more pretence in our poet. He is all for Annys, and she occasionally makes him happy. In spite of the final note, his "Invitation" is undoubtedly the offspring of a holiday humour.

>   Among the cockes of haye
>   A napkin white I spred
>   And it about did laye
>   With posies blewe and redd,
>   With sprigges of greene
>   Stucke in betweene,
>   So gay a cloath was neuer seene!
>   Nonino, nonino, etc.
>
>   I curds and creames did bring
>   And yellow juncats too,
>   Cleare waters from a spring
>   And foaming milke alsoe,
>   And manchets white,
>   And berries bright
>   Al sugred for my loues delight.
>   Nonino, nonino, etc.
>
>   I fetcht the hiuèd tresure
>   Of honie from the bee
>   Lyke sunlightes spangled plesure
>   Upon a fretted sea ;

> And plum and peare
> And peaches fayre,
> Bright globes of bursting sueet, were there,
> Nonino, nonino, etc.
>
> But when untoe the feaste
> My loue I did inuite
> She turned it al to jeast
> And wold not sup nor bite.
> To dine alone
> I was not prone,
> My joyaunce and delight were done.
> Nonino, nonino, etc.
>
> O rather than I'ld fare
> Upon Lucullus horde
> Of wines and dainties rare
> And all hys laden boarde,
> On dryest crust
> I'ld gladdelie fast
> Whereon my loue a looke had cast.
> Nonino, nonino, etc.

Let us desert the "Gyrlond" a little and turn again to the "Diurnall" which begins to bristle with dark references to "T. Waulshell." Plainly this gentleman sticks in Nat's gizzard. George seems to approve him, though we gather that Master Walsell did not at heart return the compliment, and was consumed with an honest desire to transplant his little love from her makeshift life to one of guarded comfort. And Annys? Did she love him? Remember, when Natty came she was "scare abouc fifteene somers," and young English maids are no Juliets to have their deeps so early stirred. I doubt not she liked Master Walsell very well as a grave, kind elder brother, and had been willing enough to have him if her father wished. But she certainly did not hasten the match during the time Nat was in London, acting minor parts moderately at the "Blacke-Friers playehouse," and singing minor songs prettily on the "Banckside." No, she uses her old friend as a probe to her new lover, and the wonder is, young lovers all! that ye smart under the treatment. Women's probes are their tools, they do not cherish 'em in their bosoms. Be satisfied that your mistress holds you worth the pricking; she will give you the whip-hand one day.

I think there is no doubt of Anisia's tenderness for Nat, a real enough thing between young demanding natures, though it last but a summer or so. The blossom of the tree is as genuine in its kind as the fruit

"THE SHEPHEARD'S GYRLOND"

thereof, yet the blossom may fall before harvest time.

"Shee was kynde to me last nighte," writes Nat (we are well in the latter part of the "Diurnall" now, and much matter, which must await further opportunity, has been omitted, or this paper would outrun its limits); and again, a little later: "My deare Annys went with mee to ye playing feeldes att Charyng, and we kist behynd a tree." And again: "Shee did nott laugh at me to-day." And again: "She was a litil sorrowefull and let mee comforte hir."

Why "a litil sorrowefull," Annys? For the sweetness of that comfort? Or were the brokers in? They not infrequently were. And sometimes you faced things plainly and thoughtfully.

She says to Nat, and not, I think, to probe him:—

"Master Waulshell saies thys is no lyfe for me. I shal marrie hym I supose."

Oh! cries Nat, who would give his mistress Heaven for her jointure, it is indeed no life for thee! but then, neither is the life offered by Master Walsell.

The "Diurnall" here becomes a medley of spoken words and Natty's personal rhapsodies, half of which may have been spouted on the spot and t'other half added on reflection with the pen. We can imagine the scene—Annys would-be practical, Nat on his Eros-winged Pegasus.

"Master Walsell, Nat, offers me a comfortable establishment."

"A comfortable prison! Here stand I in the wide world."

"He will give me servants."

"Need you more than one?"

"He will protect me."

"Oh Annys! I will love you!"

"Good Nat! is it enough?"

"Who lack it are beggars."

(I rather think she is in his arms by this.)

"Can we dine on it, will it clothe us? I am so weary of this hard life."

"Come away, then!"

"Whither?"

"Out on the green road."

"A white one o' winters."

"And my arm about you for a cloak."

"A draughty cloak!"

"My heart will patch it."

"How will we fare?"

"Sing and dance for our bread."

"Ah, Natty! you've tried that shift. Didst

"THE SHEPHEARD'S GYRLOND"

never go hungry on the road from Sussex-coast?"

"But what's to be hungry?"

"Wert never dog-weary?"

"One forgets all that."

"What does one remember?"

"The birds in the morning, the trees at night, the kind look of one's fellows, the young heart in one's body, the wonder of things, the wonder! Oh Annys! all the laughter was sweet, and none of the tears was bitter. Will you come?"

We know she did not.

Two more flowers from the "Gyrlond" are worth preservation before Nat's tragi-comedy developed its culminating "situation." Both urge a greater emotional earnestness than anything yet quoted.

> My deare, my onely loue, my bosomes floure,
> With laughing musicke dayly mocks my sighs,
> And I beneathe her hardly wielded powre
> Grow faint with longings that she doth misprize.
> The lyttel god wych dwells within her eies

"THE SHEPHEARD'S GYRLOND"

    Still drawes my teares—O drawe them into hir
Whose natural sun her natural fountein dries,
That sluggishly her streames of pitie stir.
    Wilt thou nott teach thy laughter how to weepe?
    Then I could teach my sorrowe how to smyle.
    The fayrest rose is shee whose bosome deepe
    Admits the heav'nlie deawes a litil whyle.
    Vouchsafe this mem'ry for my barren yeares,
    Once to haue seene thy laughter grac'd with teares.

This is Nat's single essay in sonnet form, and it is not the dignity of the mould alone that makes his wistfulness at his sweetheart's mockery ring truer here than in his previous laments on the same theme. His feelings are deepening, and we may be sure that by this time George has not failed to note and ponder the matter. In the succeeding verses emotion becomes yet a shade more tremulous.

"THE SHEPHEARD'S GYRLOND"

    Hir litil white feet,
Hir feet moe white then the black-
    thornes blossome
By noone and by nighte tred the hart
    in my bosome,
    And O! they are sueet!

    They fancie they goe
Ouer the greene of the grass alone,
They make of the hill-top theyr loftiest
    throne.
    Howe litil they knowe!

    O feet of my deare,
Much moe then the sod of the world ye
    haue prest,
Alle the waies that ye wander lye
    markt in my breast
    Farre-shining and cleare.

    My spirit has meadowes
Moe greene then the meadowes of earth
    are, my soule
Has loftier hill-tops, and ouer the
    whole
    Your feet cast theyr shadowes.

O feet of my fayre,
Thogh ye come to my hart torne and tyred, thogh ye perish
Of colde in the worldes frostie breth, I will cherish
And comforte ye there.

O feet of my may,
Thogh in frolicke ye come to the hart in my breast
To make yt your plaiegrounde, your daunce-place, your jeast,
I will welcome that waye.

O litil white feet,
Moe white and moe white then the blacke-thorne blossome,
Thogh ye come at the last
With bare thornes to trample the hart in my bosome,

I in the past
That haue beene a full springtyde made gladde of your blossome
Will still finde the touch of you wisht-for and sueet,
O litil white feet !

Now the end.

We learn from the "Diurnall" that George Peele is "some daies absent"—in Sussex, as we know, though our fated Nat does not suspect it. He supposes "one of Geo.'s prancks is toward." It is. Soon after his return Nat comes to him with big eyes and the mysteriously delivered letter signed "Jno. Wynne."

It is curt and much to the point.

"Nathaniel Dones yare a raskill. If yow do nott come home and marrie my sister I will brake my cudgell ouer yowre hedd and ende alle with my fist."

Peele congratulates Nat maliciously.

"Thou'rt in truth a happy shepherd now, Natty Downes," says he. "Thy mistress turns kind at last, Natty Downes. Thou shalt enjoy her thou'st sighed for, Natty Downes. A blessing on thee and thy Bess!"

"Ha' done!" groans Nat, and confesses ruefully that he never loved Mistress Wynne nor pretended to until the day he first met Peele.

"And, O George, she is seven years my elder and hath a wall eye!"

George chuckles, "I ha' seen it!" and Nat gapes. "Young fool," says George, his mouth humorously awry, " why in Jesu his name didst light on Mistress Wynne for a sweethaert? A dozen comelier were to hand."

Shamefacedly Nat explains the kindly notion that has resulted so unfortunately; " but I neuer didd thinck she would heare of it, nor I knowe nott how shee came to."

" Why I told her," says George, and the truth outs.

He was not, it seems, asleep to the philanderings of Nat and his lovely Annys, and they were little to his taste. So off he posts to Nat's old home to seek out Bess, that unknown cruelty, and makes her serve his turn. He takes Nat's verses with him (whether in print or manuscript is not clear), and we are left to conjecture which party was the more dumfounded—George by the lady for whom Nat professed his consuming passion, or the lady and her brother by the tale of it. Nat, who was beaten out of the village, might once have been laughed at as a match for his master's sister. But husbands are scarce for ladies of crooked looks, Elizabeth was getting on, Jonathan presumably jumped at being quit of her, and George cracked up Nat's fame and fortune with all the ardour of a poet's imagination. Both the Wynnes vow Bess's alleged denial of Nat a flat falsehood; if Nat

"THE SHEPHEARD'S GYRLOND"

says other of her he miscalls her. What! the honest name of Elizabeth Wynne bandied about the stews of London by this young cockerel? If he be making a jest of her, let him look to it! if he be in earnest, let him ask for her like a man! or Jonathan will know the reason why. This, the gist of Peele's story, explains the letter.

"And so to Sussex with thee, lad."

"But if I will not go?" cries Nat.

"Then Jonathan will come fetch thee."

"But if I run out of London before he come?"

And George, very blandly: "He is in the next room."

"God ha' mercy! then I'll run now."

Over my dead body, intimates George, planted at the door. "What, was it for nothing I brought him from Sussex and let him pay my bills by the way? Nay, Natty, thou shalt go back under brother Jonathan's arm."

"Oh!" protests Natty, "why all this, why?"

Then George turns serious and answers him. "Because, Nat, my Annys is for Master Walsell, a dull honest dog and no poet."

"What's amiss with poets?" cries Nat, very sore. "I'm a poet, thou'rt a poet."

"Ay," saith George, "I'm a poet, and thou—half an one, Nat. And therefore, why dost ask silly questions? Hast answered 'em in a breath. Natty, we poets know ourselves. We make sorry husbands, Nat."

The boy's answer for this is: "'I wold make Annys glorifiedly happie.'"

"I doubt it not—for a twelve-month," says George. "Master Walsell will keep her in sober content for all her days."

"George," says Nat, still, we picture, "between rueful and roguish," "both thou and I would choose the present twelve-months' bliss rather than the futureful of sober content."

"Ay, for ourselves," says George, "but not for our daughters. Go home, Natty Downes, and marry thy Shepherdess, or Brother Jonathan will break his cudgel with thy poll and thy poll with his fist. I have seen both cudgel and fist, and I say go home." Then he claps Nat on the shoulder something kindly, his "eie twinkells," and he adds, "Natty, shalt forgive me this one day. I never did love a man but some time I made him my victim."

And Nathaniel Downes went home to Sussex and married wall-eyed Elizabeth Wynne. We do not hear of his writing any verse afterwards.

FAITHFUL JENNY DOVE

Alack the day, alack the day
When my true love went away!
They killed my true love over sea,
And when they killed him they killed me.

I

WHEN Robert Green, my true love, went to the wars, there was but one ghost in our village of Maltby. Now there are two.

Let me tell you. Jenny Dove is my name, and when I was sixteen years old they called me the prettiest girl in Maltby, though that is not for me to say. At all events, Robert Green, my true love, thought so; but then no doubt there was never a girl with a sweetheart who could not say the same; but then it was not only Robert Green; there were others; though for me there was only Robert. And when we had been plighted three short months, he went to the wars.

But I go a little too fast. I ought first to tell you of the young Squire of Bride's Lane. We could not have told you in Maltby how far back his legend went ; for all we knew, he had always been there. Many people had seen him, so they said, but none agreed about his manner of dress —one said he wore a coat of mail, one said he wore a ruff, another a frilled shirt—so there was no judging when he had lived. But all agreed that they had heard him weeping at break of day beside the churchyard gate at the end of the lane by which all the Ladies of Maltby arrive to be married ; and as the sun came up and touched him where he leaned against the gate, he sank upon his knees beside it and melted away. For the Young Squire was a morning ghost, and that's perhaps why the details of him were hard to swear to—the black night throws them up, but seen in daylight, a ghostly ruff or a shirt-frill may be all one. I had never seen the Squire myself, never in my life.

But the day my true love left me, I rose early and met him, at his request, by the church porch, for he had a fancy to stand at the altar with me and make a vow of constancy, as binding on us both as marriage might be. We would have liked very well to be married, but our mothers would not hear of it, though I wanted but four years, and he but two, of twenty. So he thought of this vow instead, and as I said : " If love

FAITHFUL JENNY DOVE

itself is not stronger than marriage, Robert, what use is it at all?"

"Yes, Jenny," he said, "marriage lasts only as long as life, but love lasts after death."

I thought this very true, as well as very poetical. Robert was indeed a poet, and had written me some beautiful lines for Saint Valentine, and also when my linnet died.

Well, as I say, we met in the early morning in the church porch, before anybody was stirring, and as ill luck would have it the church door was locked, This dashed us very much, and we could not wake the verger, who was in charge of the key, because he was my own uncle, and particularly against Robert on account of his age, which indeed he could not help, and time would remedy.

I could only just keep back my tears for disappointment, and Robert looked serious, but was too manly to weep.

"What shall we do?" I asked, relying on his strength and wisdom.

"We will pledge ourselves beside some other cross," he answered thoughtfully, and glanced over the churchyard with its monuments.

But at this I shuddered. "Oh no! not one of *those*!"

"Then come and stand with me by Eleanor's Cross," said he, and that pleased me better. Just outside the village was one of Queen Eleanor's Crosses where her coffin had rested, I forget how many hundred years ago. It was a husband's tribute to a faithful wife, and well suited to our purpose. The quickest way was by the Bride's Lane, and as we crossed the churchyard to leave by that wicket the sun was just rising. On reaching it we both looked up together and said in one breath, I, "Do not weep, Robert!" and he, "Jenny, you must not weep!" But neither of us was weeping in the least and the sun shone bright into the lane, where Robert and I looked too late to see anything. But we had both heard the weeping. I took it for an omen, if Robert did not, but I said nothing; and we walked down the Bride's Lane to the cross-roads where Eleanor's Cross stood on a grassy mound. There we took our oath, and what better words could we find than Robert's own:

"Marriage lasts only as long as life, but love lasts after death."

We each repeated these words, and then I added a promise of my own.

"Robert," I said, "until you return to me I will come every morning at daybreak to this

FAITHFUL JENNY DOVE

Cross to watch for you; and here, where we now part, we will meet again."

"My faithful Jenny!" said he, and kissed me tenderly, and then I confess I melted into tears; but he said quickly, "Smile, Jenny, smile! You'll smile when we meet, let me leave you smiling."

So I managed to smile till he was out of sight. It was difficult, but it is wonderful what you can do.

The Wars lasted two whole years, and then the soldiers began to come back. During the first year I had had three letters from Robert, my true love, which were a great comfort to me. In the first one he said among other things, "How often I think of my faithful Jenny, smiling by Eleanor's Cross, as I last saw her. I have begun a ballad about you, or rather it is put into your mouth, as it were—the first bit goes:

Alack the day, alack the day
When my true love went away!
If he should die I will not wive
With any other man alive.

I stood there smiling in the light,
The day my true love went to fight—

but I cannot get any further with it. I would like to put in your white bonnet with the pink rose under the brim, and your pink frock with white frills, as I always see you. I think it will come out pretty if I can manage it."

In the second letter he said : " I cannot get on with the ballad, there is so much to do, but no doubt I will finish it one day."

In the third letter, which began : " My faithful smiling Jenny, do you still go every morning to the Cross ? " he did not speak of the ballad.

Of course I told him I did so, rain or fine, wind, sleet, or snow, and all the village knew of it, and sometimes one or another who was out even came by to watch me, and the lads and girls teased me, though not unkindly, but my mother called me a silly. He did not answer this letter at all.

Then as I say there was peace, and the men began to come home, but not all of them, of course ; and news took a long time coming, so there was much anxiety first, even when joy and not grief was to follow. But it is very strange how much hope there can be with anxiety, and every morning when I went to sit by the Cross, I was quite sure it was the day I would see Robert, my true love, come home from

FAITHFUL JENNY DOVE

the Wars. And every day I came away, in spite of my heavy heart, I felt that there was always to-morrow to wait for.

And so another year went by.

Long before it was over they began to come and talk to me, sometimes kind and sometimes scolding. My mother said I was a fool to be wasting my chances, the girls told me to give it up, some of the boys came wooing on their own, and even my best friend, Mary Poole, talked gravely to me.

"Jenny," said she, "the War's been over for a year, and all the men that we know of are home again, and for a whole year before that even Robert's mother had no news of him. Jenny, you cannot go on waiting by the Cross all your life."

"Oh, Mary!" I said, "I promised I would."

"How long had you and Robert loved each other?" said she. "Scarcely three months— and how old are you now? Only nineteen. Why, you may live another sixty years!"

"That would be a long marriage," I said, "but not very long for love. Oh, Mary!" I said to her, "you do not know what true love is."

"I do, Jenny," said she.

"Who is it?" I asked.

But she was silent.

"And can you, then, Mary," I said, "bid me not to go to the Cross?"

She bent her head and went away without answering.

Then my mother went to his mother, and his mother came to me.

"Jenny," said she, "you're a good faithful girl, as so pretty a girl need seldom be. I'll own I mistrusted you when you were younger, for looks like yours might catch a lord. But I'll say now, if Robert came home I'd give him to you with my blessing. But he won't come home, Jenny; and I'll give you my blessing the day you go to church with another."

"I'll wait to go there with Robert," I said.

Then for a little they left me in peace.

Just a year after the ending of the Wars, I went to the Cross as usual. It was a lovely spring morning, and the larks were going up, and the grass round Eleanor's Cross was blue with speedwell, and it was easy to be full of hope; so when, as I sat there, a soldier came limping along the road, it did not surprise me in the least. I sprang up and looked towards him, smiling with all my heart. However, it was not Robert, my true love.

He was a much older man, about thirty years old, greatly hurt by the Wars, as well as lame.

FAITHFUL JENNY DOVE

He came very slowly to the Cross and stood before me, looking me up and down. I waited for him to speak, but the words seemed hard to him.

"So you're here then, missy," he said at last.
"Yes," I said.
"Jenny Dove, are ye?"
I said "Yes," again.
"I've a message for ye," he said.
"Tell it to me," I said.
"'Tis written," he said.
"Oh is it a letter?" I said.
"Nay," he said, "'tis the end of a song."

Then he handed me an old bit of paper, very soiled, and on it was written these four lines:

> *"Alack the day, alack the day*
> *When my true love went away,*
> *They killed my true love over sea,*
> *And when they killed him they killed me."*

The writing was very bad, but of course it was Robert's.

So I smiled at the lame soldier in the light.

On my stone in the Churchyard they have cut the words:

JENNY DOVE
WHO DIED OF LOVE.

II

THE morning after my burial, I rose early as usual. During my short illness I had been obliged to miss a few sunrises at Eleanor's Cross ; it could not be helped. But after this I did not miss one ; or yes, just one—and even then, in a way, I did not ; but that will come later.

It was scarcely a week since I had met the lame soldier by the Cross, and if any morning could have been lovelier than that one, this was. I was in good time, so I took the long way over the Glebe Farm and through the village. The Glebe meadows were full of flowers. It is a beautiful thing to walk through flowers. No, I do not mean to walk among them, but to walk through them. They pass through your feet, and for a moment your feet and the flowers are one. Some of their sweetness is left in your feet from the daisies and primroses, and if your steps are happy, no doubt some of your joy remains with the flowers. In the copse I found a bed of violets, and lay on it so that I was filled from top to toe. I found it was so with all things.

Trees and hedges and houses can all be a part of you ; indeed, wherever you are, you become for that time the thing you pass through ; nothing is lovelier than a bird flying through your heart.

It was the same with people. You could be closer to them than when you were alive. It was a pleasure to run among the school children as they came out of school. I walked with my friends when they did not know it, and every day I sat in the same chair with my mother. If a person is sad you can carry a shadow away from her heart as you pass through her, and if you are happy you can leave your own light there.

In buildings, too, and things that grow, you feel whatever life has left there. I always knew when joy or pain had filled the hands that laid the stones and raised the rafters, what the lives had been of those they sheltered afterwards ; I always knew where men had quarrelled in the market, and where lovers had met in the woods. But now and then as I went about I lit upon something I could not understand—something sweeter than life, that had been left beneath a tree or in a flower. If it was a mood, it seemed finer than any mood shed from the bodies of things and creatures. Whenever I discovered it my spirit grew twice as happy as it had been, yet who or what had left it there I could not imagine.

I was glad to be a morning ghost, for it was only during my little vigil by the Cross that I could be seen, and then not by everybody; after that I was free for the day, and not visible at all, so that I could go where I pleased and startle no one. The night-ghosts are less fortunate, for, as I once said, the dark shows them up so, and it is a sad thing to be feared. Besides, for some reason which I do not know, most of the night-ghosts have sorrows. I had none. My only duty was to sit for half an hour in the morning by the Cross, smiling as the sun came up. This was all due to Robert, my true love. Thanks to him, I was a smiling ghost. None of us can escape a little duty, and mine could not have been lighter. Early as it was, a waggoner passed sometimes, and in the fine weather, if I looked down the west road, I would often see Mary Poole, crossing the pastures to turn out the cows. Many ghosts long for nothing but to be laid, but I did not wish to be; why should I? I had never while I lived had such delight in the world. I knew that had I died and Robert lived, I should have haunted the Cross only till he came home, and then I should have rested

FAITHFUL JENNY DOVE

quiet in my grave. But now that could not happen, for Robert was dead, and I would always haunt the Cross. I took to saying the little verse the soldier gave me, every morning as the sun rose. I had little enough to do, and it seemed in keeping to repeat it:

> "*Alack the day, alack the day*
> *When my true love went away!*
> *They killed my true love over sea,*
> *And when they killed him they killed me.*"

Besides, it was quite true. But I never stopped smiling as I said it. Many of the villagers said they had seen me, and one or two of them really had. And Mary Poole once heard me. I found her standing by the cross one morning when I arrived. She was looking up the road and did not see me, so I sat down behind her, and when the sun came up I said my piece. She turned and looked at me, and grew pale, and said nothing. So I sat smiling at her till it was time to fade.

The only thing was that sometimes I felt lonely. You would think this was not possible, seeing that at any moment I could become a part of a beech-tree, or a young lamb, or a crop of barley, or the busy road, or Gaffer Vine's warm chimney-corner. Still, it was so. I would have been glad of some one to talk to.

One morning in July I was a little late. I cannot think how I came to oversleep myself, but when I stood beside my headstone plaiting my hair, I saw by the sky that I would not have time to go by the Glebe and the village, where I loved to pass through the rooms of my sleeping friends. So I ran as quick as I could to the little wicket that opened on the Bride's Lane, a way I had not taken since I died. As I hurried down the lane I saw the Young Squire hurrying up it. It is a funny thing, but I had quite forgotten him till now.

They are all wrong about his dress. He wears a green jerkin, and his face is most beautiful. He is twenty years old.

When he saw me coming he waved his hand, and cried: " Jenny Dove, who died for love ? "

" Yes, Young Squire," I said, " but I am in such haste—please do not keep me now."

" Ah, Jenny, thou'rt a young ghost yet ! " said he. " How could I keep thee ? Pass, child, pass—but meet me at seven in the Withybed."

So we ran straight through each other—but oh dear, the confusion of it ! I never felt anything like it. For when you mingle with a solid body it is different ; you seem to become a part of that thing, rather than it becomes a part of you. But when you mingle with a ghost like yourself there is no telling which is which. For one instant I felt quite lost, I did not know where or who I was, or if what I had been would ever come out of that widerness. And when I'd slipped through, I was indeed not certain how much of me was left behind, and how much of him I had carried away. I was only just in time at the Cross that morning, and the half-hour went very slow.

When it was over, I went back to the churchyard to watch the clock, and at last it wanted but fifteen minutes to seven. So I thought I would go to the Withybed and finish waiting there, and I did, and as I reached it saw the Young Squire coming, too; we were both ahead of time.

We sat down together in the willow-herb, and looked at each other.

"Pretty Jenny," said he, "I have not seen thee these three months, not once since they laid thee in thy green grave. But I have heard of thee, and often found thy traces in the fields and the spinneys."

"Do *I* leave traces, Young Squire?" I asked.

"Wherever thou goest," he answered.

"And do you, too?"

"I too, wherever I go. Why, Jenny, what dost thou think? That bodies can leave their spiritual signs, and spirits cannot? Ah, Jenny, it's the spirit's spirit leaves the sign of angels on the earth—or of fallen angels."

I considered this for a while, and then a thought struck me. "Please move a little, Young Squire," I said.

He did so, and I instantly sat where he had sat. In the willow-herb, whose rosy sprays had stood within his heart, I recognised the delicate trace which had so puzzled and enchanted me wherever I had found it.

"*You* do not leave the sign of fallen angels," I said, and held my hand out to him, smiling. He laid his own on it, and I could not tell which was which.

"Jenny," said he, "these three months I have found thy smiles left wherever the spring was sweetest, and I have tried to find thee all day long. For day-ghosts are rare, and I have had some hundred lonely years. I knew it was thy task to smile at dawn by Eleanor's Cross; but unfortunately I must weep by the Bride's Wicket at precisely the same hour, and hasten to the Cross as I might at the end of my task, thou wert always gone. Let us not lose each other again, Jenny."

FAITHFUL JENNY DOVE

I told him we would not, and we agreed to meet in the Withybed each day at seven. It promised great happiness for both of us.

So ten years passed by, and we were as happy as we thought to be. For if one alone can take joy in the world's beauty, how much more can two together ! And the joy was not of the living, who fears death to-morrow ; the joy was endless, that fear was not for us.

Ghosts, I must tell you, seldom ask questions. What was, matters so little, what is, so much ; only our small daily tasks bound us for a few minutes to the lives we had left, and when those were finished we had no cares for our own, or curiosity for the other's past. Our working hours being the same, just what each did was never seen by the other, and, as I say, we were not curious to ask.

However, a few years after our first meeting it happened one Sunday that we went to church together, for it was the day I had died, and I wished to sit with my mother in her pew. And when the service was ended, and the church empty, we wandered through it looking at this and that, and by the old tomb where the Crusader and his Lady lay, the Young Squire halted, looking very kindly on the almost faceless figures. Suddenly he laughed.

"Jenny," he said, "lie there upon my Lady's effigy."

So I did as he asked, enveloping the stone form with my own, and felt strangely as he stood over me, looking down at me with the look I loved most.

"Yes," he said, "thou art fairer than she was."

"Oh, did you know her?" I asked.

"I died for love of her," he said. "I was Squire in her father's house, and we loved in secret, and my love was my passion, but hers was her pleasure. Then this knight came back from the East, and wooed her, and she was willing; and she summoned me to one last meeting, and as she lay in my arms told me with light words that this was the end. And I cried out that there might be an end to a woman's love, but there was none to her faithlessness, and left her. And the day she was to be married I sat and wept beside the wicket through which she must pass, and as the sun came up I swore to haunt that spot until one woman should prove faithful; and then I slew myself, where she and this knight found me later on. Cannot our pain make fools of us, Jenny? And so we die for love, which we should live for." He smiled at me, and we went out of the church together;

and as we crossed the graveyard he stopped beside my grave, and read the stone.

"You also died for love," said the Young Squire. "To whom were *you* faithless, Jenny Dove?"

Oh, do you know how a shadow crosses a sunny field? Would you think such a shadow could fall on a smiling ghost, as I was? Yet it did. All of a sudden I feared to tell the Young Squire my story; I feared to tell him I was faithful to Robert Green my true love, killed in the Wars. For then, you see——

I hung my head.

My Young Squire laughed at me, and said as he often did: "Oh, Jenny, thou'rt a young ghost yet! So young, thou canst still feel shame! and I'm so old that I can no longer feel bitterness. Smile, Jenny, smile!"

But if you will believe me, when he said this the tears ran down my face, and he looked at me in surprise, for he had never seen me weep before. Then suddenly he gaily laughed again, and ran in on me and stood over me, and surrounded me, so that once more I did not know myself from him, or my tears from his laughter, but in that wonderful confusion I heard his voice, merry, sweet, and teasing——

"Pretty Jenny! Smiling Jenny! Faithless Jenny!" he said, did my Young Squire.

When I heard him call me "faithless" I laughed too, and ran out of him, and he after me. It was a great game, the chase, the slipping through, the capture that could be no capture unless I wished—until such time as I did wish and stood quite still. We played that game often after this. And often he teased me for my story, and asked me what I did by Eleanor's Cross, and for what sin to love I was condemned to smile—he teased me for the pleasure of making me hang my head. But I did not weep again; why need I, seeing I had resolved never to tell him my story?

Then the tenth year passed by, and I went on a spring morning to Eleanor's Cross and sat and watched the road. And just before the sun came up, along the road, as it might have been ten years ago, came a limping soldier, of thirty years old. But this time it was Robert Green, my true love, home from the Wars.

III

As soon as he saw me he cried : " Jenny ! Jenny! Faithful Jenny ! " and came limping to the Cross. He held out his trembling hands that seemed afraid to touch me.

" Jenny, to find you here ! " he said. " My Jenny, you have not changed a hair—but you're prettier, surely ! And see, 'tis the pink gown and the white bonnet, as of old ! and see, you're smiling still ! To find you here where I left you, smiling still ! " He buried his face in his hands. " Oh, say a word to me, my love," he sobbed.

But I could not speak.

He mastered himself and looked at me earnestly.

" Jenny, I've startled ye," he said. " Yes, thoughtless that I am. You believe me dead, because I was so long a-coming—and maybe you had my message that I wrote on the battle-field when I truly thought I was dying, and gave my wounded comrade to bring to you, if he should be luckier than me. Did you have it, Jenny ? "

I nodded.

"My little love! it might have broken your heart."

"It did, Robert." They were my first words to him.

"Oh, cruel—but I'll mend it for ye, Jenny. But do not look at me so strange, see, it is myself in very faith, feel this hand, Jenny, indeed I am no ghost."

"But I am, Robert."

He looked at me as though he did not understand, then opened his arms and flung them about me, and then, poor man, he threw himself upon the ground by Eleanor's Cross with his face in the grass.

The sun came up just then, so I said my lines:

> *Alack the day, alack the day*
> *When my true love went away!*
> *They killed my true love over sea,*
> *And when they killed him they killed me.*

He lifted his face from the grass. "God help me!" said Robert Green, my true love.

"Robert," I said, "do not grieve so, there is less to grieve for than you might fancy."

"Yes, that's true," said he, "for do you remember our vow? 'Marriage lasts only as

FAITHFUL JENNY DOVE

long as life, but love lasts after death.' I need not ask ye if ye remember it, my pretty love; have ye not kept faith after death itself? Ah, Jenny, if ever a woman was faithful, you are she!"

As he said these words the shadow fell upon me, the shadow I had felt five years ago. Suddenly it seemed to me that I could smile no more. And looking over Robert's head where he knelt in the grass at my feet, trying, poor soul, to kiss them, I saw the Young Squire standing with sorrow in his eyes.

"Alas!" I cried, "what has brought you here now, when you should be at your weeping?"

"Jenny," said the Young Squire, "when I came up the Bride's Lane this morning, I felt I had no cause to weep; I leaned on the wicket, and no tears came; I could not understand it; I ran to find thee—and how do I find thee! See, with thy true love at thy feet, praising thee as the only faithful woman among women! Ah, Jenny, how hast thou deceived me!—God help me, I fear I am laid!"

He turned and fled away, and oh, if a ghost's heart could have cracked, mine would have then.

But Robert, who had not heard him, but only my question—love giving him eyes and ears for me, which no others had ; yet giving him none for other ghosts than me—Robert with worshipping eyes also answered me.

"What brings me here, but you?" he said. "And as for weeping, I'll be at that no more. See, Jenny, death need matter nothing to us ; I'll keep troth with you by the Cross each morning till I die. Even if I may not touch you, I can see and speak with you, and that half hour of love's sweet looks and words will carry me through each day. Smile, Jenny, smile, for love lasts after death!"

But I could not smile, for even for him I saw no happiness.

"Dear Robert," I said gently, "that's a vain dream. Have you forgotten to what I pledged myself when thirteen years ago we parted here? I vowed to watch each dawn beside the Cross till you returned again. Your death and my death could not break my vow—but see, my dear, you have returned, and I shall watch no more. God help me!" I sighed, "I fear—I fear I am laid."

"Jenny! you will not leave me—you will come again!"

"It will not be in my power, Robert," I said. "In a few minutes, this, my last vigil, will be ended, and I must go."

FAITHFUL JENNY DOVE

"Is there no hope?" cried Robert. "Of what use was it to come home to you, only to lose you? Oh, Jenny, is there no way?"

I thought and thought; and then, at the end of the west road, I saw Mary Poole passing to turn out the cows. Robert's back was towards her and she went without his seeing her. I thought suddenly there might be hope.

"Robert," I said, "were you true to me all these years?"

"As true as your own self," he said reproachfully. "How can you ask?"

"It might have changed things if you had not been," I said. "I am not certain—but, Robert, if you had been faithless, I might still have been allowed to lie unquiet in my grave; I might still have come each morning to the Cross, where we pledged our love; and for the sake of that broken pledge, I might have said at sunrise:

> *Alack the day, alack the day*
> *When my true love went away!*
> *My love a faithless love was he,*
> *And when he broke his faith, broke me.*

They are not such pretty lines as yours, dear Robert, but they might have served—if you had been a little faithless."

"But I was not," said Robert obstinately.

"But you might be," I said quickly.

"Never!" he vowed.

"Robert, listen," I said. "I have only a moment now. Listen with all your heart. Life is life, and death is death. You will find that death can end no love that has ever been, and that love is one and also many, and none the less true for that. Well, this is for after death. But life must be lived, not wasted. While I am a memory you still have powers to be used till you become a memory, too. And there are those you might use them with, Robert, those that need them, as you will need—theirs. Indeed, there are many powers in life that cannot be used alone. And as we find beauty, as fair and sweet not only in one flower, so we may find love as true and pure not only in one woman. Dear Robert, my time's short—promise me one last thing."

"Anything, Jenny!"

"Do not show yourself in the village to-day—let no one know you're home until to-morrow. And come at day-break to the Cross again."

"Will you be here?" he asked.

"I'll try to be," I said; and then I faded.

I did not know how it would be at all—for me, for Robert, for Mary, or the Young Squire.

But all that day I was so restless, it seemed to me I could not lie quiet in my grave that night, and if it was so with me, might it not be so with him? But I had no means of knowing, for I saw him nowhere.

Next morning, to my joy, I rose as usual. I knew I was being given one more chance. I dressed my hair my prettiest, and pulled out my frills, and tucked the rose under my bonnet-brim just where it showed its best. Then, full of hope, I sped, not to Eleanor's Cross, but to Mary Poole's bedroom.

She was still asleep. I saw how tired and sad she looked, and older than her thirty years. Oh dear, dear me! I sat down by her mirror, and pulled the little curls round my ears, and tied my sash again. Then I waked her. She did not know why she waked, or why she rose, and dressed herself, not in her old print, but her white lawn. She did not know why she stopped to gather six sweet violets and one dewy leaf from the bed by the path where they grew blue each spring. She did not know why, when she came to the end of the west road, instead of going straight across to the pastures she turned up it to Eleanor's Cross. But she knew—she knew who it was that waited there. She knew as well as I.

"Robert!" she cried, and went as white as a ghost.

He looked up quickly, but quicker still I had entered Mary Poole, who was my best friend, and stayed there, looking my prettiest and kindest at him.

"Mary!" he stammered—"I thought it would be Jenny."

Her eyes filled with tears, and she said, "Our Jenny died."

He came to her and took her hand. Oh, then I looked at Robert Green, my true love, with all my love, through Mary's tears. She never would have looked so, had she known it. Suddenly Robert took her in his arms and kissed her. How could he help it?

Then I slipped through her, through his arms, and him, so that neither saw me, and I looked at her and him; and she looked no more than one and twenty, and prettier than she had been at that age, and he looked not much older, and very tender. For, as I said, you leave what is in you with those you pass through.

I did not wait to see more—this was the one day I spoke of, when I neglected my task. I ran as fast as I could up the Bride's Lane, and there, oh joy! was my Young Squire, by the wicket, weeping his heart out.

He had just finished, as I came up.

"Jenny-all-smiles!" he cried, "why art thou smiling so? Tell me, why am I here and not resting in my grave? And why art not thou?"

"Oh Young Squire," I said, "how can I rest in my grave when Robert Green, my true love, is false to me? And how can you in yours, when I am false to him?"

I heard him say, "Pretty Jenny! Smiling Jenny! Faithless Jenny!" and then began the game of catch.

Mary and Robert have six blooming children and a little farm. It is a happy life. Sometimes they come of a morning to chat with me during my vigil, when I've nothing to do till the sun comes up, and I say my piece:

> *"Alack the day, alack the day*
> *When my true love went away!*
> *My love a faithless love was he,*
> *And when he broke his faith, broke me."*

As I said, we all have our duties, and none could be lighter than mine. Then I am free to go to the Withybed.

It is a happy life.

THE LAMB OF CHINON

" So you are going to Chinon," said Madame V., her eyes fixed on the piece of fine drawn-thread work which she did so exquisitely. " It is such a pretty town. I shall never forget it. I spent my honeymoon there, you know, and eight years afterwards I went back alone. Up at the Castle on the hill-top there was a child, a charming little boy, whom I used to go and see. His name was André Doucelin. I remember so well the first time I saw him. I had gone up to revisit the ruin, and when I had paid the old woman who lives inside the gate I heard a little voice say, ' Do you wish me to accompany you, madame ? ' I shook my head, for my desire at that time was to be alone, but after I had done so my eye caught the little figure slipping back into the shadow of the gate-house. At the same time my ear heard the tone in which he had asked the question—you know how words will sometimes mechanically reach your brain first and then be followed by the music of the voice which brings them to life. André had an adorable child's voice, so gentle and confident, like a bird. He was seven years old. When I saw his thin lively body, and his beautiful little face—he had matted tawny hair, and a pale tawny skin, all of one colour, and big dark eyes that startled you, and very mobile features—when I saw him, I felt a pang of regret at having rejected anything he had to offer. But he felt no disappointment, as I realised later. He always made his little offer to visitors to the Castle, and was contented when it was accepted, and contented when it was not. He was a charming guide. He would take your hand at once in his, and chatter away with the complete intimacy of a child who does not know what it is to be shy. However, I did not that day have him for a guide. He had retreated so quickly, and my wish to go alone through all those ruined chambers was so strong.

"The ruin is called a Castle, but it is more like the ruin of a small fortified town. There were, I believe, three strongholds, stretched along the brow of the hill, covering much ground. I seem to recall a number of separate buildings—towers, dungeons, bridges—enclosed within the ramparts set among gardens and shrubberies with trees and seats under them. A small estate. Chinon, you know, was the

THE LAMB OF CHINON 143

castle to which Joan of Arc went to seek out the Dauphin. In one of the towers, I knew, was the Chapel in which she prayed all night before she rode to Orleans, but I had forgotten which. My husband had been my guide on my first visit, but in that case I had probably listened only to his voice, and missed the information. Women do that, and perhaps you think them inattentive to you. They are, in fact, only too attentive to you, though not to what you are saying.

"When I had made my tour, I sat awhile on one of the seats in the shade of the circle of trees somewhere in the middle of the ruins. While I was sitting there I saw André pass with a small party of visitors. He was holding one, a man, by the hand, and talking eagerly; but he turned his head and looked at me on my seat, and I lifted my hand and waved to him. He waved his own hand, and then darted suddenly across to me.

"'I will soon be done,' he said, indicating the party he had left. 'Shall I come back to you then, madame?'

"'Yes,' I said. 'What is your name, my little one?'

"'André, madame.'

"'Then come back, André. I will be here."

Madame V. looked up from her work with a smile. "Why should you suffer from my old recollections, simply because you happened to mention that you are going to Chinon? I am boring you, my friend."

"No, indeed, madame," I assured her. "I wish to hear all you have to tell me of little André. Did he come back?"

"To be sure he did. He sat beside me for an hour talking of this and that. I made him paper boats and a bird with flapping wings that delighted him, and he made cocked hats of the paper, and the Eiffel Tower, and darts which he threw so that they returned to him. His fingers were very deft, and delicate like his little frame—yet his frame was agile and wiry, too. He could climb branches like a little monkey, and hang suspended by his feet, head downwards, and turn a sort of circle through his own body at a height from the ground that brought my heart into my mouth.

"'Look, madame, look!' he cried from his extraordinary position in mid-air. He was delighted at my surprise, and the expression of admiration into which I turned my fear. For you must not frighten a child with your fears for him, must you?

"I asked him: 'Do you live here?' and he

THE LAMB OF CHINON

said yes, in the holidays with his grandmother. His parents lived in Tours, where he went to school, but he liked this best. He kept rabbits here, and he would show them to me. I said, 'To-morrow, André,' for I had to go. 'Madame will come to-morrow?' Yes, I promised I would come. 'Madame will come every day?' Yes, I thought I could come every day while I was in Chinon. 'How many days?' I did not know. 'Well, I will show you my rabbits.' 'And the Castle, André—you must be my guide over the Castle. You know it well.' 'Oh, very well. I live here.' 'Do you know the Maid's Chapel?' 'Yes, of course. Did madame not see it?' 'I am not sure, André—I must have been in it, but I did not know which it was.' 'But did madame not see the Maid?'"

Madame V. drew her threads in silence, then resumed.

"He really thought he saw the Maid herself. Perhaps he did. Who knows? He spoke of her as a good friend. I asked him what she looked like, and he seemed puzzled. 'She is a woman, like madame,' he said. 'Was she in armour?' Oh no, in a dress, like the women in the fields. Had she a halo—a light round her head? No. Yes, once. It was when his rabbit was sick.

His grandfather said it would die. In the night he could not bear it, he got up and went to the Chapel and called for the Maid, and she came and sat all night by his rabbit, and in the morning it was better. There was a light round her head then.

"I went back next day, and every day afterwards during my visit. I took lunch with me, and walked in the grounds with André, or sat with him under the trees or in the embrasures of the castle windows looking down on the town and the river. André climbed the stones and walked along precipitous edges like a cat, but though it always made my heart beat faster I knew he was perfectly safe. Not only was his confidence his safety. I felt he was being watched.

"He showed me his famous rabbits, and among them the big lop-eared one that had been saved by the Maid. He did not speak much of her, except when I referred to her, any more than he spoke of his schoolfellows in Tours. On the other hand he did not appear to be reticent about her. She knew how to handle a sick creature, he said, she was used to handling her father's lambs. 'She often looked after the lambs,' said André.

"During my mornings there I sometimes saw

THE LAMB OF CHINON 147

the old grandfather tending the flowers and paths. The grounds were his job, and there was a vegetable garden in one part. The grandmother attended the gate, and the sale of postcards on a stand opposite her doorway. The room these three lived in was a queer one—just the old stone chamber that had been the gate-house, dark like a cavern, but with a little fire lighting up the medley of pots and furniture, and the faces of the old people, and André's playing on the floor. Behind this, in a part of the grounds which tourists did not trouble about, as it had no remains of the Castle on it, were sheds and a woodstack, and André's rabbit-hutches.

"The old grandmother became friendly, and sympathetic. She had noticed my black dress, and asked if I had children. 'One can see madame loves children,' she said. I said it was easy to love André. 'Yes,' she said, 'many people who come here are fond of him. He spends all his holidays with us. He is delicate, and a little fanciful.' She made no more direct reference to his imaginations about the Maid.

"André, of course, had soon shown me the room in which she spent her night in prayer. I did not ask him whether he saw her there then, and he did not mention her name except to explain something as he might have done to any of the visitors he led through his familiar haunts. Sometimes he shared my picnic, and on one hot day I had brought lemons and a syphon with me. He was very interested in the syphon, and liked to press the lever. When we had made the drink, I asked him, 'Would you like some, André?' 'I don't know, madame.' He tasted it, and I had to laugh at the comical way in which his little face puckered into a sort of agonised smile. 'That pricks, that pricks!' he said, laughing as soon as he could. After that I brought syrup and bottled table-water—you know how bad the ordinary water is in most places.

"He got sous from the tourists every day, but I never gave him money. I said I would bring him a toy; what would he like? He answered instantly, 'A steamboat—a steamboat that goes on the water.' I thought of the funny cheap bazaar down in the town, and said, 'I am afraid there's not such a thing in Chinon, André.' 'There is in Tours,' he answered. Then I knew he had in mind some special toy he had once seen, on which his heart had ever since been set. 'Where?' I asked him, and he vaguely described the shop and the locality.

"Later on I searched the bazaar and found, of course, nothing."

"Poor little André! he had to do without his steamboat, then."

Madame V. drew her threads with a faint smile.

"No, he did not do without his steam-boat. I went to Tours and got it."

"You went to Tours! A long journey for a toy. You must have been very fond of André, madame."

"I was. Dear me, my friend, where are your ears? Have you attended to nothing I have been saying? But is it not strange? that journey to Tours ended it. I might have stayed on in Chinon for ever, for I was living, not by days, but in a certain state of being. The little trip to Tours broke up that state. I grew restless, my grief came back, and in a moment everything was changed. As the train drew into Chinon I knew that I could not bear to be there any longer. The very feeling that had driven me there was now driving me away. It had become too painful. I drove to my hotel and told them I would be leaving in the morning by the first train. It was then evening. I went at once to the Castle, to give André his toy. I had been away two days, as I had had some trouble in finding the shop.

"When I rang the bell at the gate, the old

woman came peering with her finger to her lips and tears running down her face. 'Oh, it is you, madame!' she said, seizing my hand.

"My heart almost stopped beating, as I asked, 'What is the matter?'

"'André, he is ill—he is dying—the doctor says he cannot live through the night.'

"Would you believe it? In that short time he had taken the fever and sickened, my little André. The old grandmother wrung her hands and whispered, 'Madame, he calls and calls for the Maid. He says his rabbit is sick, and she can make it well'—my friend, excuse me."

I was silent until she was ready.

"Then André died, madame?"

"No," said Madame V. with her tender smile. "That is the beautiful part of it. He got better. Well, well, all that is fifteen years ago."

"And you saw him often afterwards?"

She shook her head. "You will think it strange, but after his illness I never saw him again. I couldn't go back to Chinon. It was perhaps weak of me, but I couldn't bear it."

Madame V. laid down her work. "You'll stay and dine with me," she said rising. "Please. Excuse me while I dress."

During the evening we talked of other things. At parting she said, "If you go up to the Castle

THE LAMB OF CHINON

—but of course you'll go up to the Castle. And of course there will be nothing. How stupid I am. A good journey!"

Chinon is, as Madame V. had said, a pretty town. It is more than that, it is delightful. I was not prepared for so much charm, for madame's heart had been on the hill-top, not on the river-bank. But when I mounted to the Castle I was quite prepared for all I found, even for the aged woman who opened the gate to me. There was, however, no child in the doorway of the dark old gate-house, and no little voice to ask, 'Shall I accompany you, monsieur?'"

I paid my fee, and wandered for some time among the ruins and the grounds, which I felt I was visiting for the second time. But like madame at her second visit, I wondered which was the Maid's Chapel. I had not discovered it when I came upon a vegetable patch on which a man was working. I looked, expecting to see an old gardener, but this was a young one, in his early twenties. Approaching him, I said, "Can you tell me which is the Maid's Chapel?"

The young gardener turned to me. I thought I had never seen anything so beautiful as his face, or rather, as the look he gave me. There he was with his tawny hair and pale tawny colourless skin, his strange dark eyes, so dark that they had an immense depth, and the gentle smile on his young mobile mouth. It was the eyes and the smile that moved one so.

"Yes, monsieur," he said, leaning his rake against a tree. "I will show you the Maid's Room. This way."

I went with him across the gardens.

"Is not your name André Doucelin?" I asked.

"Yes, monsieur."

"You live here?"

"Yes, monsieur."

"With your grandparents."

"My grandfather is dead, monsieur."

"He used to look after the grounds."

"I do that now. This is the Maid's Room." He stepped in ahead of me, then turned back with that strange gentle smile.

"Yes, it is all right. Come in."

I went into that dark primitive chamber, expecting to see I know not what. I wondered what André Doucelin saw. Unable to restrain my curiosity, I said, "Did you think some one was here?"

"She might have been."

"The Maid?"

"Yes"

"You see her?"

"Every day, monsieur." André Doucelin smiled at me. "She saved my life, you see, when I was a little one."

"The Maid did—really?"

"Yes, monsieur. I had the fever, the doctor said I could not live, but the Maid came and sat by me all night with her hand on me. She was used to her father's lambs, you see. She had a light round her head. She brought me a boat."

"I see," I said. "Thank you."

"It is nothing, monsieur." André Doucelin led the way into the sunlight again, and went back to his garden. As he took up the rake he said, "My grandmother will show you the boat if you ask her."

"I will, as I go out."

The young man gave me his beautiful smile again, and I left him raking the earth.

At the gate-house I bought some postcards, and when I had paid for them, said to the old woman, "I have been talking to your grandson, madame."

"To André, monsieur? He is very gentle, quite harmless, they would not let him be here otherwise, and what would I do without him since my husband died? He has such a way with the flowers, as perhaps you saw."

"Was he always like that?"

"Well there, monsieur, who can say? He was always a fanciful child, but no more than that, we thought, till after a bad illness he had when he was seven."

"Yes," I said, "I've heard all about that."

"He told you?"

"A little. But I am a friend of Madame V."

At the name the old woman broke into exclamations. "Madame V.! Monsieur is a friend of madame! Ah, monsieur, how glad I am to see you! How is she, the dear madame? She is a saint, monsieur! We owe her André's life."

"How is that?"

"She came when he was at his worst, when the doctor swore he could not live through the night. He had been calling for the Maid to come. Madame sat down beside him, kissed him, and laid her hand on his head, and he was quiet at once. She showed him a boat she had brought him—shall I ever forget his face? He fell asleep with it in his arms. Madame never stirred from his side all night. If he moved or opened his eyes she stroked his hand and spoke to him so gently, so gently, till he slept again. In the morning he was calm and quite cool. The doctor said it was a miracle. But of course she should not have kissed him, the dear madame."

"Why, what happened?"

"She took the fever herself. She lay a long time ill in Chinon and was moved to Paris as soon as it was possible. We always hoped to see her again, but we never did. She wrote to ask—what do you think—to adopt André. But what would you? he was his own mother's only child, and she could not let him go. Besides, he was touched, we knew it by then. Is she well, the dear madame?"

"Yes, quite well."

"She had lost her husband. Did she console herself?"

"She never married again."

"What a pity! such a beautiful lady. And she should have had children, monsieur, she loved them so much! See, here is the boat she gave André. It is his greatest treasure. He thinks it came from the Maid. After his illness he never spoke of Madame V. again, only of the Maid. We did not like to tell her how it was with him, we thought we would wait till she came. But she did not come, I don't know why."

Ah, Madame V.! Perhaps it was weak of you, but you could not bear it.

THE TOMBOLA

1

THERE was to be a Fête Nautique one Sunday in August in a gay little town on the Vienne. The attractions, posted up for two weeks beforehand, were numerous; rowing races of all sorts between the nautical clubs from the neighbouring Departments, a Tombola with two hundred prizes, donated by local magnates and shopkeepers, music in the evening under the trees on the river-bank, fireworks, and a prize for the prettiest illuminated boat that appeared on the water at night. The market men and women who came in every Thursday from the surrounding country read the announcements, and carried back word of them to the villages and farms. Gaspard Tournay, driving his mother back to their farm the Thursday before the Fête, presently said:

"*Mère!*"

Gaspard was not a talker. The work of the farm among the animals and the furrows was easily carried on by grunts and ejaculations: "*Hé!*", "*Ho!*" and "*Heu!*" in varying tones—

the horses and the oxen understood these well. When words were wanted for business purposes, Gaspard could say those that were to the point, could tell the blacksmith to shoe the mare, or a customer the price of potatoes per kilo. His mother did the bargaining. But to find speech for an announcement of any kind was hard to him. His young, rather uncouth, rather attractive face, with its slightly Tartar setting of brows and cheekbones, and a heavy lock falling limp over the right temple, was dumb and sulky like a goat's; but his dark eyes looked out between brows and cheekbones with a sort of muted question, and his glance, that shifted from side to side, could never stay upon another person's eyes. Perhaps his only moments of real communication were those when he pulled his dog's ear and said, "*Hé, toi!*" The dog then sprang up at him to lick his face, and he uttered a short rough laugh, and pulled its ears. It took Gaspard half an hour's cogitation before he was able to bring forth that difficult, "*Mè...*"

His mother glanced sharply at him.

"Well?"

"I shall go to the Fête."

"What's that? *You'll* go to the Fête?"

"Yes."

"On Sunday?"

"Yes."

"And the work?"

"I'll make that up."

"And the money?"

"I've ten francs saved."

"Saved indeed! And for what? To squander!"

They drove on a couple of kilometres.

"*Mère!*"

"Well?"

"Would Madeleine go?"

His mother gave him a sharper glance than before.

"Perhaps. That's for her father to say."

"Ask him, mother," said Gaspard with an effort—his last.

His mother did this for him without protest. She went across that evening to old Leroux, and told him, with some nodding and chuckling, what Gaspard proposed. Leroux nodded and chuckled, and agreed. These two owned more land than any one else in the village, and they wanted to see it run together. But Gaspard wouldn't speak, and Madeleine wouldn't help him to. Her father scolded and petted her, his mother nagged at Gaspard, and nothing happened.

"He means to settle it on Sunday," said Madame Tournay.

"If she'll go," said Monsieur Leroux.

He asked his shy daughter if she would like to go to the Fête. Madeleine threw her arms around his neck.

"Do you mean it, father?"

"Of course I mean it. Why not? Aren't the Fêtes made for pretty young girls like you?"

"And nice old men like you!" said Madeleine, hugging him.

"Oh, me! That's another story Gaspard will take you. Go and enjoy yourselves."

"Who?" Madeleine's arms slackened.

"Young Tournay; enjoy yourselves."

She withdrew her arms entirely. "I won't go with Gaspard."

"Come, come, you won't? Then you won't go at all!" her father scolded her.

Madeleine flushed. "And how do you know he'll take me after all?"

"His mother says so."

"His mother! No, I won't go with him. You must take me."

"Not me, my girl. You'll go with him or none."

Madeleine knew when her father was past coaxing. During the preparations for supper and the clearing of it, she said no more. After supper, however, she got out her straw hat, that she only wore when she went to town, and pulled the blue ribbon this way and that. In the morning Leroux put his head through Madame Tournay's door and said, "She'll go."

"Good!" said Madame Tournay. At dinner she said to Gaspard, "She'll go."

Gaspard said nothing.

II

On Sunday he and Madeleine drove in to town. He was in his working clothes, with a clean blouse, and Madeleine wore a blue cotton dress, the colour of chicory. Her round arms, her neck and cheeks, of the smooth warm tint of a brown egg, were set off by the blue of her dress, and her eyes looked out from under the straw hat, full of anticipation. Gaspard's, as usual, glanced sidelong with their unasked, unanswered question. But what did she anticipate? She had no idea. And what was his question without an answer? He did not know. They were no help to each other. He promised nothing to fulfil her eager mood, she nothing to solve his dumb problem. After their exchange of greetings when she mounted the cart, they drove between the fields of vines and corn, and through the flowery woods, in silence.

But when they came to the lively little town, Madeleine could not contain herself as they drove through the narrow cobbled streets, whose ancient timbered houses had hung out coloured rags and flags for the people, as centuries ago it had hung out cloths of silk and gold-fringed velvet to welcome kings. The little white square with the fountain in the middle of the green acacias was full of ribbons, wreaths, and streamers, and in the market-place a red-draped platform stood, with four big discs full of numbers displayed upon it.

"Ah, how pretty it is, how pretty it is!" said Madeleine several times, not particularly to Gaspard. He made no response, but drove to an inn where he could put up his horse. While he did this Madeleine stood in the market-place, gazing, and when he returned she addressed him for the first time.

"What are those, Gaspard?" She pointed to the discs on the platform.

"I don't know."

They began to move away with the gathering crowd; peasants in their best and also their worst, shopkeepers and their families, respectable and comfortable, gentry in smart light-coloured clothes.

There were several girls in yellow, pink, and blue dresses, with hats to match. Most of their arms were bare, nearly to the shoulder, and they all had bangles on. They looked like flowers, Gaspard thought, but their dresses! you could almost see through them. His glance shifted quicker than usual from side to side, but still he caught gleams of colour, and heard laughter and chattering—like a lot of birds in a cage, he thought. "They're young ladies, too. How busy they seem, busier than anybody, they're running about on their high heels, but what are they busy about? What shoes! Heu! hasn't that one any stockings on? Yes, she must have, the silk glistens on her instep, but it's the very colour of her feet!"

"Would you like a programme for the Fête Nautique?" A charming-looking schoolboy in a fresh white blouse accosted him. The boy had a pile of green programmes in his arm, and held one out to Madeleine with a smile.

"Thank you." She took it.

"It costs a franc." The boy smiled at Gaspard.

"Oh——" Gaspard gasped. A whole franc out of his precious ten for a bit of printed green paper.

Madeleine looked at him. To her, too, it

seemed a great deal, but still—wasn't he going to do anything?

"Thank you," she said again, and handed back the programme. The boy did not mind a bit, but ran on and offered it to some one else.

On the corner of the street running down to the river, a big café spread itself over the two angles of the road. A striped awning was stretched above the drinkers, and a circle of shrubs in tubs attempted to confine them, but to-day the chairs and tables had broken through, and spread into the road. People sat drinking coffee and Byrrh, and sipped various coloured syrups through long straws.

"Let's drink something," said Gaspard suddenly. He gripped his ten francs hard in his pocket. If a bit of green paper cost so many sous, what would a red or a yellow drink cost? But he had said it, and they sat down. The waiter came. Gaspard did not know what to say. Madeleine said "I like grenadine." "And you?" said the waiter. "Grenadine," said Gaspard.

It was very sweet. It was good. He sipped slowly, watching the other drinkers under the awning, and the passers-by in the dazzling sunshine. Madeleine watched too. It was all so gay, so confusing. They did not speak, and he looked one way, she another. They had all but forgotten each other.

Through the drinkers pushed a nosegay of flowers—a girl in green muslin, one in yellow silk, and one in white with black-and-cherry ribbons and a cherry-coloured hat. They fluttered little books in their fingers, and merrily addressed the drinkers at all the tables, whether they knew them or not.

"Tickets? Tickets for the Tombola? Thank you, m'sieu. You? Tickets? How many? No more? Ah, this next one is a lucky number, take it! Thank you. Tickets? You have some already? But that doesn't matter, have some more, you can't have too many, no doubt you've not bought your lucky number yet! No? Thank you, madame. A ticket, m'sieu'? Thank you!"

One of them was near his table now, the one in the cherry hat, glancing her eyes over the customers for likely purchasers. Her glance reached him—it rested on him—it met his uncouth peasant look of suppressed interest and inquiry. She was smiling at him, straight into his eyes! He couldn't look away, for the first time in his life.

"A ticket for the Tombola?"

How pretty she is! Her arms are quite bare

to the curve of the shoulder, in full daylight, too. There's a dimple under the gold bangle above her elbow. It must be her party-dress, for it's cut low on her neck, and the gold chain she wears dips under her bodice a little as she leans over his chair. The black and pink ribbon isn't round her waist at all, but tied higher up. How round and pretty she is!

"You'll have a ticket, won't you? They're only a franc. Such lovely prizes—you've seen them in the shop-window of course? This is a lucky number, it has two sevens and a nine on it, it will win you the bicycle, I'm sure. Thank you. And one for mad'moiselle? Such lovely prizes. She would like the lace shawl, I'm sure. Thank you."

She was gone, with her red lips, and lovely blue eyes and dark lashes, and the wonderful smooth colour on her cheeks, and the smile that for one moment had belonged to *him*, and the musical voice that had spoken words to *him*, and the sweet scent he had smelt as she leaned over *him*.

In his hand were two bits of paper with numbers on them: 5779, 5780. He offered the second one to Madeleine, who had turned round during the purchase.

"Here's yours," he said.

THE TOMBOLA

"Thank you. Shall we go and look at the prizes?"

They finished their syrups, and found their way to the shop that was displaying the two hundred prizes in its window. Yes, there really was a bicycle and a grand lace shawl; there were bottles of scent and wine, packets of cigarettes, hair combs and pipes, a fishing-rod, a statuette, a necklace of pearls, penknives, a pair of pink vases hand painted with pansies and ornamented with gold, an inkstand, a cannister of tea, many coupons bearing shop-keepers' names, and saying: "Good for a Chicken"; "Good for a Cake"; "For a Kilo of Butter—for a Shave—for a Dozen Eggs." They could not take in all the prizes.

"See how many things there are!" said Madeleine, with flushed cheeks. "We might quite likely win something. Oh, what a splendid shawl!"

Gaspard stared at the lace shawl and the pearl necklace. How lovely she would look with the lace round her beautiful shoulders, or the pearls hanging down on her white breast.

III

EARLY in the afternoon the rowing races began. Gaspard and Madeleine took up their stand at the starting-point. The winning-post was far, far away up the river, a long walk in the burning sun, and there was less to see there than at this end, where the crews came along the bank, carrying their boats before launching them. They passed so close that they sometimes brushed you, these heroes, and you could hear their voices, and see their muscles, and the different colours of their costumes : white and blue, black and red, black and yellow, red and blue. They were a race of gods from Nantes, Saumur, Angers, Tours, dark, fair, and auburn, sombre and smiling, smooth-skinned and hairy. One in particular they noticed, a red-gold youth in green and white, with a fair skin, fierce and merry eyes full of light, a quick way of talking, and a face like a laughing lion. He dominated his comrades, and threw a spell, in passing, over the spectators. Madeleine did not remove her eyes from him as he sprang into the boat and took his oar, and rowed into position in midstream. Doubtless others in green and white rowed with him, but she did not see them.

THE TOMBOLA

The gun went off, and the boats were away. Smaller and smaller they grew till they became mere specks on the wide sandy river. Presently they could be seen no more. Nobody seemed to care much about the result. They watched the preparations for the next event. In time rumours blew round vaguely that such and such a race had been won by Saumur, by Loiret, by Nantes, but Gaspard and Madeleine asked no questions, had no programme, and did not know the names or colours of the crews. They watched all that happened near them, however. Presently the leonine hero reappeared for another race, the double-sculling championship, with only two entries. It was green and white against red and black. Green and white drew quickly ahead, and led till they were out of sight. Before the result of this race came back, the spectators on the banks began to drift away. They had watched the rowing desultorily for two or three hours ; that was enough. Madeleine and Gaspard drifted with the others back into the town.

IV

THE populace was collecting in the marketplace, getting as near as it could to the platform with the discs. On the platform stood the Mayor, one or two ladies, a group of girls, and several gentlemen. Four young men stood behind the four discs and whirled them in turn. An arrow in each paused at a certain number, and when they were stationary the numbers on the discs were called out from left to right by the Mayor.

"2143!"
"0765!"
"1148!"
"0029!"
"3085!"

And so on.

As the Mayor called out the numbers a man beside him noted them in a book. They were the winning numbers in the Tombola, every number indicated by the arrows had won a prize. The prizes themselves were not named; no doubt they were all in the clerk's notebook. Gaspard soon got the hang of it. When the arrow on the first disc pointed to 5, hope leaped in his breast. Now surely he was to win the pearls, or the lace shawl! But no. The second

THE TOMBOLA

disc had stopped at 2, and his hope sank back again.

The announcing of the numbers took a long time. Before it was over some people left their places, and others pressed up for better positions. Gaspard always manœuvred to get a little nearer. But Madeleine, after an hour, found it dull. It began to get dark, flares were lit around the platform, and the monotonous numbers, still announced regularly in the Mayor's flat voice, had lost meaning and expectation. But Gaspard stood rooted, staring at the fateful discs.

" 0622! "
" 1983! "
" 5——" (Ah!)
" 7——" (Ah! ah!)
" 21! " (*Oh!*)

Madeleine pulled at his sleeve. "Gaspard!"
He took no notice.

She was hungry and bored. Was he going to stand there for ever? What had they come for? To hear M. le Maire pronounce those interminable numbers, hour after hour?

The kaleidoscope of the crowd shifted again. Madeleine was jostled aside by the press, and she put out her hand to hold Gaspard's arm. "Gaspard!" The man she held said: "*Excusez!*" It wasn't Gaspard. Ah, there he was, three lines away, moving off through the thick of the crowd. At last he was going to get out of it. She pushed after him as best she could, but lost him for a moment on the outskirts, and then saw him going quickly towards the river. She ran after him, calling : "Gaspard !" He turned. "*Excusez, mademoiselle !*" It wasn't Gaspard. The coat and hat were exactly alike.

She hurried back to the market-place. The crowd was breaking up. The draw for the Tombola was over. She couldn't see Gaspard anywhere.

V

They told her at the inn that Gaspard Tournay's horse was still there. She asked if she might wait till he came.

"As you please. But it is barely eight o'clock. The dancing and the fireworks will go on till eleven. He will not come before it is over, and you'll be missing all the fun. Go down to the river where the band is. He is sure to be there."

When you are shy, and at a loss, you accept any lead. Madeleine believed that she would

THE TOMBOLA

find Gaspard where the band was, and had she not believed it would not have liked to remain three hours at the inn after being advised to go. But she returned to the river, and followed the left bank where it ran by groves of trees, with wide spaces here and there where people were dancing, and moving among the gay booths. There were open booths that sold sweetmeats, cakes, and trinkets ; others, mysteriously closed, where you might see a sword-swallower, or consult a fortune-teller ; still others, where young men shot at whirling pipes, for the fun of the thing. Near the statue of Joan of Arc the band blared out its music, just as the booths flared out their lights, without seeming to affect either the quiet or the darkness of the groves just beyond them. They splashed their immediate neighbourhood with harsh flames and sounds, but penetrated no farther. The dark under the trees seemed darker because of the garish booth-lights, and the quiet still quieter for the distant band-tunes.

Nowhere could she see Gaspard. She had only a few sous in her pocket, and she bought a couple of little cakes to appease her hunger. She felt forlorn. Clapping hands and cries of admiration drew her to the riverside. There, in mid-water, floated a golden ship. In the darkness you could see nothing but the lights, which outlined mast and rigging in gleaming lines upon the night. You could not even see the occupant, or if it had one. It floated as by magic up and down the river, like a fairy craft. It was more exquisite than anything Madeleine had ever dreamed of. One or two other little boats, hung here and there with red and blue lamps, or displaying paper lanterns, appeared at different points. People said : " That's pretty!" " See, there's another ! " and were delighted when a lantern caught fire and had to be extinguished. But these little boats brought no illusion with them, you knew they were the common boats from which Jacques and Jean fished daily in the Vienne. The little golden ship was an enchanted stranger, and might have sailed down from the stars. Watching it, Madeleine forgot her loneliness. Presently it floated out of sight under a bridge.

She recommenced her search among the crowd; in vain. Farther and farther through the trees she wandered, leaving the outskirts of the town behind her. Now she began to feel sore towards Gaspard. He had no right to bring her to the Fête, and then desert her. She might have been dancing, and she had no one to dance with. He might have been buying her beads, or treating

THE TOMBOLA

her to sweetmeats, or taking her into the fortune-teller's tent to learn her fate. And having learned her fate, he might . . .

Tears welled to her eyes and dropped down her cheeks, as she stumbled through the soft sand and grass beside the river. She was now some distance from the town. She had passed the Octroi without noticing it, and found herself wandering quite alone, with the water on her right hand, and on her left the low willow copses which formed little bays and peninsulas on the sand. Behind the willows lay the unseen meadowland, and through the shadowy leaves came the scent of flowers. The moon was full on the water, the shining shallow water that ran swift as a swallow over its golden bottom. She had heard that in some places you could wade from side to side of the wide river with the water never higher than your armpits. The night was hot, the water was like crystal flecked with gold, the stars lay in its bed like diamonds, and it was so still, so still and beautiful. Where the river lapped the shore the sand heaved up in tiny islets, so that near the edge you might step from one to another, while the water ran between in little channels. Even in midstream it was so shallow that the sand heaved here and there, like the curved back of some wallowing golden beast.

Madeleine went into a willow-copse, stooped down, pulled off her shoes and stockings, and leaving them among the trees ran back to the water and stretched out her foot. No, it was not cold, it was delicious. She lifted her skirts to her thighs and went forward, laughing softly. She trod from one isle of sand to the next, stepped down into the lightning current, and felt it fight against her calves as she waded round the next willow-copse. There, with a gasp, she stopped. Before her lay the golden ship, wedged in the sand in a green bay of leaves. Its occupant was pushing vainly with an oar against the sandbank.

"*Holà!*" he called, as she appeared. "Come and lend a hand. I am stuck." Then, as she moved into the fairy light, he said, "Oh, pardon, mademoiselle! I thought you were a man."

Madeleine stepped round the willows on to the shore, and let down her skirts. "Perhaps I can help you," she said. "I am strong."

He looked at her splendid peasant figure, and as she turned up her blue sleeves admired her fine round arms, as a moment before he had admired her fine legs.

"I don't know this reach of the river," he said. "I come from Laval. I did not know

THE TOMBOLA

how shallow it was beyond the bridge. Can you push from behind?"

Madeleine pushed, to little purpose. Then he got out of the boat, and pushed beside her. His red-gold lion's head bent close to hers. She could feel his shoulder, in the white jersey with the green band, leaning to hers in its thin blue cotton. As they pushed side by side, she asked shyly, "Did you win the race?"

"What race? We won some and lost others.

"I mean the single race against the man in red and black."

"Yes, I won that. You were there, eh?"

"Yes, monsieur. I saw you," said Madeleine.

The boat budged.

"There!" he cried. "Now once again! Bravo! she's floating."

He jumped in, held out his hand, and pulled her in beside him before she knew what was happening. "Thank you. You're as strong as a boy. Let me sail you back to the town."

Sail! sail with him, the blue-eyed lion, the hero of the races, sail with him in the golden ship past all the people! The dark would hide her from their eyes, as it had hidden him from hers. She looked down at her feet and stammered, "My shoes and stockings."

He laughed. " Where did you leave them ? "

" Among those trees." She pointed.

" I'll fetch them. Keep the boat steady, don't let her drift on to the sand."

He sprang out of the boat and waded ashore. As he disappeared into the copse she felt the current taking her, and cried out. He came running back, splashed through the stream, and clambered into the boat, dropping shoes and stockings at her feet. She put them on while he steered carefully through the deeper channels till they reached the bridge.

Back again to the people, the tall black trees, the booth-lights and the band. As the golden ship floated once more into sight, she heard the cries and clapping on the banks as from another world. Now she was a part of the enchantment, the part the people could not see. She and he together.

" Yours is the prettiest boat on the river. You'll get the prize," she said

" Do you think so ? What is your name ? "

" Madeleine Leroux."

" Where do you live ? "

She told him.

" If I get the prize, Madeleine, I'll send it to you."

" Oh no, monsieur ! "

THE TOMBOLA

"Oh no, monsieur? Oh yes, mademoiselle! Or shall I bring it, eh?"

"Oh, monsieur! to sail in your boat is pleasure enough. Thank you. Shall I get out here?"

"No, no, there are the fireworks beginning. See!"

On the farther bank dark figures crouched among the trees. A flare, a hiss, and a snake of fire reared up, and burst in coloured stars above their heads. The crowd on the town side broke into a shout.

"Oh! they are falling on us!" cried Madeleine, afraid and happy.

But the coloured stars melted in mid-air before they reached her.

VI

GASPARD was waiting for her at the inn. His horse was harnessed, ready to be off. As she came up he said, "We missed each other."

"Yes," she nodded.

Both were a little dazed. They rode home side by side, as silent as they had ridden out. They did not really see each other. During that ride she only saw a young god in white and green, with splendid shoulders, bright hair, and fiery laughing eyes. And Gaspard saw a vision in white and cherry-colour, with red lips, bare arms, and a round bosom.

In Madeleine's thoughts the words ran round and round : " Oh yes, mademoiselle ! I'll send it to you. Or shall I bring it, eh ? " In Gaspard's ran the numbers : " 5779 ! " announced in the Mayor's tired voice. 5779 had won a prize in the Tombola. The last but three, it had won a prize. What was it ? The lace ? The pearls ? He had hurried to the shop. It was shut fast. People were staring through the window at the rich array. He said to some one, awkwardly, " I've won a prize."

" *Hein ?* you're lucky."

" But the shop is shut."

" Yes, of course it is. The prizes can be fetched away to-morrow."

" But I must go back to the farm."

" Then next market-day. The prizes won't run away."

Next market-day he'd fetch his prize, and present it to her. He knew who she was, she had been on the platform talking to the Mayor. Some one had said she was his daughter.

"I'll see her on Thursday and give her my prize!" thought Gaspard; while Madeleine thought, "He'll bring me his prize, and I'll see him again."

VII

MONDAY passed. He did not come.

Tuesday and Wednesday passed. He did not come.

On Thursday the thought of him began to fade like a bright dream. Had that strange hour by the river, that hour in the golden ship under the coloured stars, been true? Life was what it always was, not what it had seemed to be that night.

Thursday was market-day. Gaspard drove the cart for his mother. She was in a bad humour with him, had been, indeed, since the morning after the Fête. She and Leroux had met and nearly quarrelled about it.

"Nothing has happened."

"Nothing has happened."

"Hasn't your fool of a boy a tongue in his head?"

"Can't your stupid girl give him a sign?"

At home, however, the parents turned their vexation on their own.

Gaspard had not told his mother of his luck. He knew well enough what she would think of his giving away, to a strange girl, the treasure fortune had bestowed upon him. As soon as he could he slipped away, and presented himself nervously at the shop. The window was three-parts stripped of its display. The pearls and the lace shawl had both been taken. But many dazzling prizes still remained. His tongue clove to his palate and he could not speak. He showed his ticket. A woman examined it and looked it up in a list.

"5779—yes, that's a winning number. The vases. Here they are."

She fetched from the window the wonderful pair of pink urns, with gold rims and gold scrolls for handles, and the bunches of pansies painted on one side.

"My felicitations, monsieur !"

"Thank you, madame." Gaspard took the magnificent vases awkwardly, and went out with them. How beautiful they were. He must not let his mother see them. He hurried to the Mayor's house, so fast that he had not time to realise what he meant to do. But when he got there he stopped aghast. Where would he find

THE TOMBOLA

the courage to ring that bell and ask for the young lady? It was impossible. What could he say? How explain himself? Into what terrible position was he about to thrust himself? Should he leave them on the doorstep and watch till she came out? If only she would come out now!

The door opened, and she came out, she herself. She was with one of her friends, and they looked different; they wore coats and skirts, and though they were smiling and chatting with one another, they did not seem to be the girls who on Sunday had smiled and chatted with all the world.

They passed by Gaspard, standing mute with his gaudy vases in his big hands. The Mayor's daughter glanced at them, but not at him; she made some laughing remark to her friend, and they turned the corner.

It was over. She was gone, and the vases had not been given. They could never be given now.

He trudged back to his mother. She began to scold as soon as he came in sight. "Where have you been? Isn't there enough to do that you must make yourself scarce? *Mon dieu!* what have you there? What have you been spending good money on?"

"I spent nothing. I won them."

"You won them? How did you win them?"

"At the Fête. In the Tombola."

"*Mon dieu*, what fortune! You won them! What did you pay for the ticket?"

"One franc."

"One franc, for those two vases! That was a bargain, my boy."

"Yes, mother."

"What are you going to do with them?"

He did not answer.

She glanced at him shrewdly. "Well, put them under the seat in the cart where they won't break."

He obeyed, and the rest of the day took its usual course. But in the evening when they reached the village, she made him pull up at Leroux's gate.

"There's Madeleine in the garden. Go and give her your vases," commanded Madame Tournay.

Gaspard got down slowly from his perch, and brought the vases from under the seat. He went through the garden carrying them in his hands. Madeleine looked up, and stood still, watching him. He came and stood beside her, half looking at her, half looking away from her, with the shifting glance in his eyes under its loose goat's-lock. She waited for him to speak, and at last was obliged to help him.

"What beautiful vases, Gaspard. Why—they were in the Tombola!"

"Yes. My prize."

She looked astonished. "Not really? You won a prize in the Tombola?"

"Yes."

"You didn't tell me."

"No, I—didn't know what it was."

"How pretty they are!"

"For you."

"For me? You're giving me your prize?"

"Yes."

He put them into her hands. To his surprise her eyes filled with tears. She turned her head away. Gaspard looked at her uneasily, then suddenly he cried, "*Hé, toi!*" as he cried to his dog whom he loved. She turned, and fell against him. He gave a short gruff laugh, and fondled her ear.

Madame Tournay drove round to the back to find Monsieur Leroux.

THE RED APPLES

ARNOLD had left the boat half-way between Rouen and La Bouille. He had already been once to La Bouille, and exhausted it. Pretty as it was, set out on its shelf over the water at the foot of its hill, it had the air of pointing a finger to itself, common to places that depend largely on pleasure-seekers. It was the Mecca of the little steamboats that plied to and from Rouen three or four times a day; and it knew it. Arnold had been more attracted by half-a-dozen of the little landing-places on the opposite bank, and when Nan and her party proposed another excursion, he agreed on conditions.

"I'll get out half-way and walk," he said. "Come too, Nan."

"It's so hot for walking," she objected; "besides, we couldn't possibly get to La Bouille in time for lunch."

"Who wants to? We'll take sandwiches and picnic on the way. The country is so perfect, with all those orchards."

"But all the landings are the wrong side for La Bouille. How could we join the boat again?"

"Ferry across from Sahurs. Do, Nan!"

"I don't think I will." She knew her own tastes, and liked lunching in a restaurant balcony over the river, and pottering among souvenirs. Arnold sometimes had his faint doubts of her.

"Well, I shall, anyhow."

"You'll spoil the party."

"Nonsense. I'll enjoy it in my own way."

"You ought to be more sociable."

"Sorry," said Arnold, in a tone that meant he wasn't.

Somewhere between eleven and twelve o'clock he left the boat at one of the floating landing-stages. As he crossed the high narrow bridge to the shore, one of his party called after him: "Don't forget that the last boat leaves La Bouille before five."

"If you miss it," added Nan, "you'll have to spend the night in your orchards."

"I shan't miss it," he cried. "I'll be at La Bouille in time for tea with you."

"He'll want it," said Nan two minutes later. "He has left his sandwiches."

Arnold did not appear at La Bouille in time for tea. The last boat began to pack itself. The English party in the first-class settled itself fretfully.

"It isn't as though he hadn't plenty of time,"

THE RED APPLES

said one. " He oughtn't to dawdle, putting us out like this. You'll have to teach him not to be irregular, Nan."

" It's his own business," said that young lady coolly.

The boat let out the prolonged hoot that meant departure. As it died down a shout was heard from the middle of the river. The passengers, French and English, leaned over the rails. From the Sahurs bank the ferry-boat was approaching. Its five or six occupants stood up in it, shouting, gesticulating, dancing. The young ferryman doubled and straightened himself as though his life depended on it. One figure only sat calm and smiling in the flat craft, Arnold himself. The peasants about him shouted to the distant steamboat, and waved their arms, like shipwrecked mariners sighting a sail.

" Stop ! stop ! stop ! "

" They see us ! "

" They do not see us ! "

" Yes, they see us, they see us, ah, they stop ! "

The steamboat had, in fact, recognised the efforts of a belated passenger to reach it. It took the human, not the official, view of the situation ; on the point of motion it checked itself, and consented to leave La Bouille three minutes late. But the peasants in the wherry still danced and shouted, the ticket-collector on the steamboat danced and shouted in reply, and the ferryman still strained his muscles to bursting-point. Another minute and the ticket-collector slid back a section of the boat-rail, leaned down, and hauled Arnold aboard as though he were rescuing a drowning man. Arnold flung five francs to the ferryman, and the steamboat moved up the Seine. Everybody was well-pleased except the English party, towards whom Arnold made his way, laughing.

"Pouf! that was a narrow squeak. What a jolly to-do they all made!"

"It was very conspicuous," said Nan. "What made you so late? Hadn't you plenty of time? Where did you get that apple?"

Arnold looked thoughtfully at the beautiful dark-red apple as he answered: "Yes, I'd time enough, but I got in a bit of a fix. Would you like this apple?"

"No, thank you, I've just had tea, perfectly dreadful tea. You didn't even have tea, I suppose? What sort of a fix?"

"Well, a sort of—police-fix."

"Arnold! how disgusting! what happened?"

"I was accused of stealing."

"Stealing what?"

"Apples—red apples."

"Arnold ! no wonder if the French don't think much of us when we come abroad."

"Hold on," said Arnold. "I took the only way of keeping the peace, and preserving pleasant relations between France and England."

"What way ?"

"Open confession."

"You confessed to it ?"

"I was caught red-handed, you see."

"Do you mean you really *had* stolen the apples ?" demanded Nan, looking at him with indignant eyes.

Arnold turned the apple in his hand reflectively.

It was exceedingly hot at midday, walking on the flat side of the Seine between the orchards. Cornfields, dotted with fruit-trees, kept in by neither hedge nor fence, strayed to the edges of the road, their fringes blue with scabious and cornflowers, in which unseen grasshoppers kept up a harsh incessant whirring. Here and there a nobleman's small park stretched its short length between the crops, shady and rich, but walled in ; a fanciful iron gate was soon sure to appear, and reveal a wide drive leading to a flat-faced ornamental house, looking like a villa in an old print, or one of the models children cut out of cardboard thirty or forty years ago. Sweeter were the orchards, red and green with apples ; with cows hobbled in the grass, and hens attending them ; and in the middle of the trees a thatched barn or a little house, with a peaked witch-like roof projecting over one end of its timbered walls. An orchard in a fairy tale, thought Arnold, with some magic girl or crone for its occupant. But nobody appeared as he walked, either on the road between the cornfields, or behind the wrought-iron gates of the Marquis, or at the queer little windows of the witch-huts among the apples. The day was at full heat, and the time was the hour of rest, when French business stops like run-down clockwork.

He had turned inland from the flowery river-banks, and no longer knew where he was. It did not matter. Time, work, life as he knew it had ceased ; only appetite had not. He found a path that lay between the forbidden greenwoods of some baron, and lay down under a tree. Then he discovered the absence of his sandwiches. So he filled his pipe and smoked awhile.

He wandered on, in search of a village with a café. Villages there must be, for those floating landings on the Seine had names ; but he could

THE RED APPLES

find none, and no one to ask. He had turned too deep into the pastures to begin with, and the villages lay nearer the banks. At three o'clock he made a turn which he thought must bring him to the river, if he pursued it straight; but it led him first to a green tree-shaded meadow in which stood, on one side a great fantastically-lovely barn, on the other a small timbered farmhouse; goats and poultry, calves and horses, wandered through the grass between the two like their possessors. Otherwise the place seemed to lie asleep in the sun. So beautiful was it that Arnold stepped inside; nothing had ever broken him of his belief that all beauty was made for his enjoyment.

The moment he entered a spell seemed to snap. A couple of peasants appeared at the barn door and gazed at him doubtfully, from the farmhouse issued a man and a woman, the woman big, gaunt, with hard cheek-bones and a sour mouth, the man a trifle shorter, but broad and stocky, with a dark intelligent mistrustful face. He came within barking distance of Arnold.

"*Vous voulez ?*"

It was difficult to explain in limited French. In any tongue, perhaps, the mere quest after beauty is difficult to explain. Arnold spread his hands vaguely and answered: "*Pour le plaisir de regarder !*" He smiled illuminatingly at the black-browed farmer.

But the farmer did not light up. "*Allez-vous-en !*" he barked, and Arnold knew himself suspected.

He retreated from the private paradise, determining to take the first public path to the river, which he was sure could not lie more than half a mile away.

Before long he found a path, but it pushed its way between fields that seemed half-private. On one side stood a small house, retiring from the pathside under its trees in the usual fashion of these Norman cottages.

"Perhaps I'd better ask," thought Arnold, and stepped up to the cottage. Some one moved inside. He cleared his throat and said : "*Pardonnez-moi !*"

The inmate came quickly to the door. She was a young woman in a pink cotton dress and a white apron ; twenty-five, perhaps, but with the perfectly innocent look of a young child. She had a sweet pleasant face, a clear rosy skin, very blue and open eyes, and very fair hair, quite lovely where the sun touched it. She smiled at Arnold with a complete lack of shyness.

"Monsieur ?"

THE RED APPLES

Arnold smiled at her, and summoned all his French. "*C'est par ici la route à la rivière? Je veux aller à La Bouille.*"

"Oh, you are Eenglisshe!" she said in that tongue. She stepped out of the cottage and went on in her own language. "Yes, it is there, I will take you to it."

"Oh, you mustn't trouble; tell me, I shall find it."

"I like to come, I like company, I will show you." She motioned him into the path, and walked beside him, beginning to chatter like a confident child. "I was with an Eenglisshe lady two years in Nice——"

"You're from the South?" Arnold looked at her Northern yellow hair.

"Oh, no, I am from Caen, but I live with this lady two years at Nice. Then she go home to Ollande Parc, and I come back here and get married. It is very lonely sometimes."

Arnold paused to peer over a hedge into an orchard with blue flowers in the grass—he always peered over hedges and through gaps for what he might see there. She waited uninquiringly while he looked.

"Lovely!" he said.

"The apples? You like apples? I give you some, I have good apples."

She turned promptly and began to retrace the way to her little house. Arnold found himself following her.

"I say, no, you mustn't really, you're too good."

She smiled at him. "I like to. My apples are very good to eat. I like to."

In a few minutes they were at her door again. She motioned him to wait, disappeared, and reappeared quickly with two handfuls of dark-red apples, beautiful to look at, sweet to smell.

"You put them in your pockets. They are good."

"What beautiful apples!" said Arnold.

"Yes, they are a pretty colour," she smiled, "and they are good too."

She turned and trotted once more down the path. Arnold wondered whether he ought to profit by so much simple willingness. He hurried after her and said, "Why should I bother you like this? I'm sure I can find the way."

"Oh, no, I will show you. It is not quite easy. And I was alone, there is no work to do, and I do not see many people. And it is good to help when one can, isn't it? Sometimes I see nobody all day."

THE RED APPLES

"It was livelier in Nice?" smiled Arnold.

"Oh, yes, there were people there."

"Your husband works all day then—are these fields his?'

She laughed merrily. "Oh no, oh no! we are not like that, we are not rich enough to have fields. My husband is——" The word escaped Arnold, he could not gather what her husband was. "Sometimes he goes about the country all day long on his bicycle, and I do not see him at all. But he does not like me to see people much, he is very good, but he is very jealous, so many people do not come to see me now. He makes such scenes!" She shook her head. "It is because he loves me."

"And you love him?" said Arnold. It was like asking a child if she loved her doll.

"Oh, yes! but——" she laughed, "I do not make scenes. When he begins to be jealous his face grows quite purple, and his eyes disappear, and quite ten lines come in his forehead—it is all for love, of course. Then I put my hand on him and say, ' Dear silly!' and if I do it in time he grows quiet, and it is all right."

"But if you don't do it in time?"

For an instant the smile died out of her clear child-like eyes, and under the rosy colour her cheeks grew pale. Then she shook her head quickly. " It does not matter so much. It is all right presently."

They had been walking and turning as she chattered on, crossing a ditch lined with a noble screen of poplars, and now they stood on a path at the bottom of a field stacked with haycocks, big and little. Only a thick fringe of loose-strife and meadowsweet waved between them and the flowing Seine. She stopped as soon as they reached the footpath.

" You know the way now," she said. " The ferry is to the left, at Sahurs."

Arnold fumbled for words. None seemed to fit the parting that had come on him as swiftly as the meeting.

" You've been so kind," he said. " The apples——"

Her candid eyes checked him. As though she wished to stop him from offering what would hurt her she took his hand.

" I like to give them to you," she said simply.

" Then—thank you." He shook her hand, with a firm clasp. They smiled straight into each other's eyes, and then she turned and went up the hayfield, passing behind the cocks. He stood still. When she had gone a little way she turned and waved to him, and he waved in response. In a short while she turned again, and

THE RED APPLES

the waving was repeated. Seeing that though she moved he did not, she turned at frequent intervals, growing smaller and smaller between the cocks, until she was at last only a pink dot in the distance. Arnold tied his handkerchief to his stick, held it high, and waved it till she was invisible. Then, completely happy, he strolled along the river path in the direction of the ferry, feeling the apples in his pocket.

The scent of them reminded him sharply that he had eaten nothing since his morning coffee and roll. There was still plenty of time to catch the boat, and tea with his friends had lost its attraction. On one hand was the flower-bank of the Seine, on the other, hemming him in, the Norman orchards. A gap in the hedge invited him; he dropped through, stretched himself under a tree, and ate first one red apple, then another. The child-like woman was right; her apples were very good.

But as he set his teeth in the fifth he got a shock. He was seized and shaken to his feet, and irate speech hurtled round his ears. The speaker was no other than the dark-browed farmer on whose lands he had trespassed earlier in the day. The details of his voluble wrath were beyond Arnold's powers as a linguist to translate, but the thesis was clear enough. He was accusing Arnold of stealing apples from his orchard.

Arnold protested vigorously that the apples had been given to him.

The farmer laughed harshly, and pointed overhead.

Arnold looked up and beheld a tree laden with red apples, precisely like the one in his hand. He shrugged his shoulders, and suggested, as well as he could, that these were not the only red apples in the world.

The farmer glowered, and indicated that these were the only red apples in Sahurs. From the flow of his speech Arnold detached some disjointed words that bore on his previous trespass at the farm. He retorted with heat. The farmer retorted with greater heat. Arnold signified that he had to catch the boat at La Bouille, and had no time to waste. The farmer sent him, his boat, and La Bouille to the devil, and the incoherent dispute took a new turn. Words redolent of the police, the law, crept in, and Arnold realised, with some dismay, that the farmer was going to be really nasty about it. He had Arnold by the collar, and was insisting on hauling him before the police, for stealing his red apples.

THE RED APPLES

The alternatives of fight, flight, and compensation presented themselves to Arnold, and were rejected. He said curtly : " *Laissez-moi ! Je viens avec vous.*" The farmer removed his hand reluctantly, and Arnold walked beside him up the orchard, then up another, then across a pasture, then into the identical meadow with the barn which an hour ago he had encroached on from the opposite side.

As they crossed it the dour woman came out of the house, and asked her husband a question. He replied rapidly, explaining that he had a thief in tow.

Arnold reflected on the absurdity of the situation, but as he saw his accuser taking the road he had himself pursued after his banishment from the farm, it occurred to him that an easy acquittal lay at hand. In two minutes they would pass the cottage of his innocent guide. He would ask her to testify to his own innocence.

To his surprise the farmer himself turned into the field in which the cottage stood, and shouted a name. A figure came once more to the cottage door, a figure clothed not in pink and white cotton, but in official male apparel. The burly figure, then, was not only the local policeman ; he was her husband. His broad face beamed with bonhomie.

The farmer put his case. He had found the English monsieur under his red apple-tree eating red apples. The monsieur said he had been given the apples. That was all *blague*, for as everybody knew there were no such other apples in Sahurs. Here was the very apple, with the mark of monsieur's teeth in it. The policeman, who had listened good-naturedly, addressed himself to Arnold.

"Who do you say gave you the apples?"

But before Arnold could reply the policeman saw the apple in the farmer's hand. He snatched it, examined it, and his face underwent a complete transfiguration. It turned quite purple, his brow was corrugated with a dozen lines, his eyes practically disappeared in his head.

"*We* have such another tree!" he roared. "*Who do you say gave you these apples?*"

The noise brought the child-like woman running to the door. She looked at her purple husband with a smile, laid her hand on his arm, and said: "Dear silly! w ~ is it?" Then her glance fell upon Arnol and the farmer, and took in the red apple in her husband's hand. The smile died out of her eyes, and her face grew pale as Arnold had seen it do before.

THE RED APPLES

"Who gave you the red apples," shouted the policeman for the third time.

Arnold saw the good relations of France and England eternally endangered. He pulled himself together, smiled guiltily, and answered: "Nobody. I confess. I was hungry. I saw the apples in the orchard. And I took them."

The purple melted from the policeman's countenance as from the clouds at sunrise; his brow smoothed itself, his eyes reappeared. At the same time the colour stole back to the little woman's cheeks, and her eyes smiled pleadingly —but at neither Arnold nor her husband.

The policeman turned genially to the farmer. "Well, there it is! He confesses. It is no such great matter, just a few apples. But it is your affair."

Arnold looked at the farmer to read his fate. Over this man, too, a singular change had come. His dark face, cleared of anger, was left unexpectedly kind and quizzical. He answered: "Let it pass. As you say, no such great matter, only a few red apples." He held out his hand to Arnold. "Put it there!"

Arnold put it there. The policeman nodded, took his wife's arm, and re-entered the house. Arnold and his late accuser walked down the road together to the farm.

"She's too good for him, the little woman," said the farmer, "a child like that! One day his passion will go too far. I never knew they had a red apple-tree—he keeps things to himself, my faith, yes! If you want to catch the boat, run down through my meadows, it is the nearest way. But run past the back of the house, you understand. If my wife sees you she will ask questions, and want to know why I have let you go. And it does not always do to tell the truth, my faith, no!—as you understood, monsieur, when you confessed to stealing my apples."

He laughed, shook Arnold's hand again, and pushed him off with a gesture of secrecy.

"Do you mean," demanded Nan, "you really *had* stolen the apples?"

Arnold, turning his one remaining apple in his hands, reflected that there was only one way of preserving pleasant relations and keeping the peace. "Well, yes," he confessed, "I had. I was hungry. I saw the apples in the orchard. And I took them."

FIRING THE RUSH

FIRING THE RUSH

Elsie had never known the country till that Easter. Not the real country. Her limited suburban life, sheltered for nineteen years by parents, had included conventional holidays by the sea, and an occasional day at Epping or Richmond. Then her parents died and left her without either material or spiritual independence. She had to find a post and earn her own living. She was shy and timid and pretty, and not very competent at anything. But after a struggle she got a clerk's post that did not call for experience, and was poorly paid. She went unprepared into life, and she did not understand the men and the girls she worked with, but especially the men. She got through the work always shrinking or scurrying a little.

Then came the Easter week-end in that unbelievable spring when even in London the March days felt like May and June, and the flower-sellers' baskets were full of primroses, wild daffodils, and palm. The girls in the office talked of the long week-end holiday, from Thursday evening till Tuesday morning, and how they would spend it. Elsie, having no money for seaside lodgings, had no plans. But on Wednesday she heard one of the girls say to another, " Mother's ill. I can't go."

" What a bore for you. Where were you going ? "

" Bigham, to a farm I know. It's awfully cheap, and they give you cream with your porridge, and you can get on the top of Bigham Down in half an hour and see the sea. I expect the marsh marigolds are all over the watermeadows now, and you never saw such woods for violets and anemones. It's too late to cancel. I was going to-morrow night. Look at the weather, too! I could have picnicked all day on the Downs, you can't think what it's like up there, and it's always so jolly coming back at night to a big supper. You take your meals with the people who keep the farm, you know. I do feel sick about it."

Her talk ran on intermittently through the morning. Elsie's work was shot with glimpses of flowers and rivers and Miss Rounce's homemade cake and butter, and the joys of gathering eggs and feeding chickens, and the cow the disappointed girl was going to learn to milk. " Mr. Rounce promised to teach me. Him and I are great friends." It sounded like a picture-book story to Elsie, especially the woods where you could really pick anemones. She hadn't known before that anemones grew wild like buttercups and daisies.

At lunch time she moved over to the girl whose mother was ill and said, "Did you say it was cheap?"

"What was cheap?"

"Your farm you were going to?"

"Yes, a pound for the four days—that's for everything, including a goose-feather bed. Miss Rounce stuffs her own."

"Is it far?"

"Bigham? Not much more than forty miles —it's Sussex, you know."

Elsie made a silent calculation. She thought she could manage it. But she was so unused to swift resolves that it seemed like some other Elsie's voice asking, "Could I take it off you?"

"You?"

"Your room—could I go instead?"

"Oh, rather! Yes, of course. Yes, that would be splendid. I'll let Miss Rounce know. You get the 6.25 to-morrow evening from Victoria—it's a through train, and the carrier will meet you. You ask for Mr. Worth and say you're for Rounce's. It's four or five miles from the station, and Miss Rounce will have supper for you. It's an awfully jolly joggety ride in the dark. Shan't I wish I was you at half-past eight to-morrow night!"

At half-past eight on Thursday night Elsie was jogging in the carrier's cart to Rounce's. She looked at the starry sky, on which the stars seemed to be ringing, so much more sharp and silver were they than any stars she could remember, and she saw the bright paring of the moon hang low behind the silhouettes of the big elms; she heards birds call and wings make movements that were strange to her, and she smelt the Sussex night, the smells of the flowery lanes, the water-meadows, and the wind off the Downs, whose soft masses against the sky-lines she took for banks of cloud. She got out of the cart, when it stopped, in a sort of dream.

The next days did not break it. She discovered that the country of the picture story-books *was* true—that daffodil fields and anemone and primrose woods *were* true, and the life of the barnyard, the shepherds and the dog that folded the flock at evening, the Downs, the trees, the river, and the great water-meadows golden with celandine and dun-coloured with rush, soft like the sides of a Jersey cow—these things *were* true, not only to be looked at but intimately lived with! To think that one could pick the daffodils by handfuls, skirtfuls, unforbidden, that one could go alone on the lonely hills, eat lunch up there beside a dew-pond, dip one's face and wipe it in the short sweet springy grass, lie on one's back and look giddily at a vision of the miles of land below, pretend to read, and drowse, drowse in the hot sun. And then, if one dared, one could go at milking-time into the stalls—if one dared. On the first night, over supper, when, not quite at ease, she had been making talk with the Rounces about her friend from whom she had taken the room, Elsie had said to the farmer, "Miss Lawrence told me you'd promised to teach her how to milk a cow."

"Yes," said young Mr. Rounce, "I believe I did. I shall have to teach you instead now, shan't I?

For two days Elsie lived a little in dread of this offer. She was timid with cows. She was timid with many things: timid of the silence on the hills, of trespassing in woods, of treading the narrow planks across the dykes that drained the water-meadows, the treacherous planks that bounced at your second step. She was timid of a gipsy in a lane, and of the night. Not of the dawn. The air at sunrise, the larks rising in spirals, the dew on all things, made her laugh like a child and catch her two hands together under her chin. She wanted to kneel and pray and thank God, but was too shy to. But to be out alone at night !—yes, she tried that, too. She wanted to know what it would be like on the top of the Downs at night. She set out bravely, but a hundred yards from the farm was filled with fear. She went on between the copses of birch and oak and pine, with stars in every puddle of every cart-rut, she ran in little spurts and made herself reach the foot of the borstal up the Down. Everything got big and silent and strange on the hillside. She laboured up, her breath coming shorter and shorter. Before she reached the top she passed between two hawthorns, and a wind sprang up so that they rattled and chattered at her. Then she turned and ran, and ran, like a hare. She got back panting, but recovered her courage at the farm-gate. It wasn't more than ten o'clock. Young Mr. Rounce was smoking by the fire, and his sister, who was fifteen years older, was bustling before bedtime. Young Mr. Rounce glanced at Elsie as she came in, quick-breathing, with her soft dishevelled hair and flushed cheeks.

" Been strolling ? " said he.

" Yes," said Elsie. " I went a little way up Bigham Down."

FIRING THE RUSH

"Oh, did you?" said young Mr. Rounce. He glanced at her again.

"You'd better not go doing that, child," said Miss Rounce brusquely.

"Why shouldn't she?" said her brother.

"You never know what sort's out at night. You'd not catch me alone up there."

"I did get frightened," confessed Elsie. "I ran home."

"Oh, did you?" said young Mr. Rounce again. He had a grave and very pleasant voice, with a slightly bantering undertone. He was still better to look at than to listen to, of a beautiful lean build, and his movements at his work were as good as the movements of all natural things, horses at the plough, sheep-dogs running on the hills, birds flying, branches in the wind. Elsie, herself unnoticed at the edge of the field, had watched him for an hour that morning, sowing seed broadcast. She did not know what held her watching him so. She thought she was reading her novel. But a buried sense within her was responding unconsciously to the rhythmical beauty of his going and coming, of his easy walk and the scattering action of his arm and shoulder.

"Well, you'd better not go alone again to Bigham," remarked young Mr. Rounce, "unless

you take me with you. Susan," he said, knocking
out his pipe, " I shall fire the rush to-morrow."

" What, Easter Sunday ? " cried his sister
scandalised. " Don't you be so godless ! What'll
the neighbours say ? "

" What the neighbours choose," said young
Mr. Rounce. He stretched his arms. " When
did I care what the neighbours say ? "

" I wouldn't boast of it," said Miss Rounce.
" They've had cause to say plenty."

" Shoo ! " laughed her brother. " You'll be
frightening Miss Morton again, and she'll be
running up Bigham faster than she ran down.
The rush has to be fired some time, and to-
morrow 'll be dry."

" Don't you do it. The Lord won't prosper
it."

" Well, I'll think about it."

" And think better of it," said Miss Rounce.
Then they went to bed.

On the staircase the farmer said to his sister,
" She's got quite a bit o' colour to-night. She
was a pale little piece when she came."

Young Mr. Rounce did think better of it,
but not so well of it as to accompany Elsie and
his sister to church for the Easter service.

" I'll go to service to-morrow night," he said,
" at Sparrow's."

"Yes," snorted Miss Rounce, "and much good you get of those services at Sparrow's!"

She went on grumbling a little, but more from habit than hope. She knew her brother by now. He was a young man, who without neglecting his crops or his beasts, carried everything he did in an easy-going manner that had the appearance of laziness. Yet under his quiet bantering voice and slow quizzical smile he kept a fund of vitality which, in ordinary intercourse, threw out sparks in tones and glances, and, on given occasions, blazed into flame. He could drink or dance most of a night with men or girls, and be at work with a clear eye before any of his carters. But he was still in his youth, twenty-six at most. The neighbours shook their heads and said, "Wait till he's his sister's age, then we'll see if he's half the man she is."

At the evening milking-hour he invited Elsie to the dreaded lesson.

"Let be till to-morrow," counselled Miss Rounce.

"If we let everything be till to-morrow," said he, "what'd get done to-day? Mustn't the cows be milked now?"

"Of course they must," said Miss Rounce, "but there's no call for you to go converting Miss Morton on an Easter Sunday."

Mr. Rounce addressed Elsie in his grave warning voice. "Don't you come, Miss Morton, if you're afraid of the parson."

"Oh, but I'm not," said Elsie, blushing a little. "Only I—I expect I shan't be able to do it."

"We're all beginners some time," he said, and they went to the stable. "You shall try on Daisy. She's going dry, and you can't spoil her."

Elsie entered boldly at his side, and he watched her under his eyelashes as she placed her hand with forced confidence on Daisy's flank. He saw that her fingers trembled a little, and he smiled with the corner of the mouth she couldn't see. He felt them tremble still more, as he showed her how to close them on the teats. Daisy was as mild as a tabby cat, but when she turned her head and looked at the new milkmaid with her red-rimmed eyes, or when she flicked her tail, Elsie could not help saying, "Oh!" She said it again when, after her first few ineffectual efforts, the milk suddenly spurted anywhere but in the pail. Young Mr. Rounce, who was kneeling beside her, laughed quietly, and wiped his cheek with his hand. "There now," he said, "it's all over your pretty Sunday blouse. What a shame."

FIRING THE RUSH

Elsie looked at him nervously; she had grown very rosy and her eyes were full of tears.

"Oh, I really can't do it, I—I really can't," she stammered.

"Why, that's all right," he said gently. "Some folk try a week and don't do that much." He took out his big handkerchief and dabbed her blouse and neck.

"Please, you do it," said Elsie in a muffled voice, and got up hastily and left the stall.

Monday was the hottest of all those hot spring days. In the morning, when Elsie was going round the barnyard with Miss Rounce collecting eggs, she stood up suddenly and sniffed.

"Something's burning!" she exclaimed. "Oh, and see all that smoke over there on the water-meadows."

"It's the rushes," said Miss Rounce calmly.

"But is it all right?"

"Of course it's all right, child; Jim's firing 'em."

"Oh, yes, he said he was going to. Why is he doing it?"

"They're no good to man or beast. No good for thatching, and spoil the grazing."

"They're so soft and pretty, though."

"Yes, they're pretty enough, but they do the ground no good."

"Will they grow again?"

"In no time. You can't stop 'em in that sort of ground."

"Isn't the fire dangerous? mightn't it spread?"

"Not past the dykes. You see how they cut the meadows up in squares. Jim's firing it square by square. Did you speak to Worth about fetching you, child?"

"Yes," said Elsie. "He's coming very early to-morrow, about half-past five. You see, if I get the six-fifty I can have breakfast at Victoria, and be at the office easily by ten."

"I'll have a bite for you here before you go," said Miss Rounce. "It don't do to travel on an empty stomach."

"I wish I weren't going," said Elsie.

"Well, you must come again, child," said Miss Rounce. It's done you a sight o' good. You look twice as pretty as when you come."

Elsie laughed, and coloured up. "Then I must certainly come again." She took Miss Rounce's hand rather shyly. "Oh, of course not because of that. But you've been so kind, and I've liked it so much."

FIRING THE RUSH 223

Miss Rounce patted her hand, and they finished getting the eggs.

At dinner-time Miss Rounce said to her brother, "You got your fires going nicely."

"It's the right day for it," said young Mr. Rounce. "I shall start another bit or so this afternoon."

"Miss Morton was asking questions about it this morning."

"She'd better come down and look on."

"I'd like to," said Elsie.

He went down earlier than she. When she closed the gate of the yard behind her, and stood on the top of the slope that ran down to the water-meadows, she could not see him at first, though here and there the slow thick columns of smoke drawled through the shimmering air. It was indeed a shimmering day. Small cycles of midges were dancing in the haze and shine. Elsie went slowly down the slope, and stood gazing across the green and brown of the smoking meadows to the Downs, which looked very soft and distant in the heat. She looked at it all, longing never to leave it. The whole world shimmered like a dream.

Presently young Mr. Rounce came up to her. He had seen her standing there for some while. He came quietly, and she did not notice him until he was quite close.

"Couldn't you find where I was?" asked young Mr. Rounce.

She shook her head without looking at him. "No."

"I'm doing the bit beyond the withy bed next," he said. "You come along and help me."

They went side by side without talking, crossing the squares of meadow by the improvised bridges over the dykes. Each square had its entrance at one corner, but to traverse easily the whole of those rich acres you had to know just where the entrance was. Jim Rounce did not smile when she hesitated to trust herself to a plank, but gave her his hand and helped her over with a strong haul. She noticed by eye and touch the power of his brown hand and the moulding of his forearm, she noticed the way his hair was streaked on his damp forehead, and the fine shape of the dark head and set of the neck. He had a rush between his teeth and was whistling softly through it. To break a rather long silence, she asked, "What tune's that?"

"Murphy's Two-Step. Know it?"

"No. Do you dance?"

"Yes. I like it. Do you?"

"Scarcely ever. I don't know much about the new dances."

"Oh, you ought to," said young Mr. Rounce.

"Here we are now. The plank's rather shaky—take my hand."

They stood together in one of the farthest of the water-meadows. He stooped to his kindling. She was alive to every one of his natural and beautiful movements, to the shimmering of the day, of her heart, as a pale flame flickered ghost-like in the sunlight, and then was smothered in the rising smoke.

"It only smoulders, you know," said the farmer. "I'm afraid you'll be disappointed if you wanted a blaze."

"I don't think I wanted a blaze. I just wanted to know what it's like."

"That's what it's like. Now you know," he smiled. "I'll go across and start that other corner, then we'll get out."

He went across rather quickly, and she began to follow him slowly, in her dream. Then he heard her utter a cry of fear, and turning saw her running rather aimlessly into the smoke; beyond her, driving her towards it, was the plunging form of one of his horses.

"Curse it!" said young Mr. Rounce, "how did that happen?"

He ran between the girl and the horse and caught her arm, pulling her back.

"Don't be frightened," he said in his quiet

steady voice. "Stay here where you are, and don't get the wrong side of the smoke. I'll have to get Captain round and out of this. I didn't see he'd got grazing here, and he's afraid, you see. Now don't move, please."

She remained quite still, and he went up to Captain and soothed the trembling horse in much the same accents as those he had used to soothe the trembling girl. He put his hand on its neck and led it round the fire, and sent it across the dyke into the unfired grass. Then he came back to Elsie, who stood exactly where he had left her.

"All right now?" he asked gently.

She looked up at him, her face pale, her lips very faintly smiling, her eyes full of wonder, and at that moment a small bush near the rushes caught and burst into flame hissing and crackling. The wave of heat and extra light startled her into a second cry—a low one—and the colour flowed over her cheeks, and the eagerness and fear in her eyes took fire. She trembled violently. Jim Rounce put his left arm round her, and she felt herself tightly held. She could no longer see his quizzical attractive smile for her eyes were hidden against his shirt, but she knew his head was bent close to hers, and she heard his gentle bantering voice murmuring through her hair.

FIRING THE RUSH 227

"Why, you're afraid of everything, aren't you?" he was saying. "You're afraid of the cows and the horses and the parson—you're afraid of the dykes, and you're afraid of the dark, and of the fire, too. Is there anything you aren't afraid of? You're afraid of *me*, aren't you, you silly little thing—aren't you? aren't you? Are you afraid of me?" he whispered. "What are you afraid of?" She felt his lips on her hair, lightly at first, then pressed closely into its soft loose wave. He put his right hand under her chin and turned her glowing face up to meet his mouth. "What are you afraid of?" he whispered as he kissed her again and again. Scarcely knowing what she was doing, Elsie put her arms about his neck and kissed him too.

She heard him say, "We won't fire any more of this to-day, it's getting late." Keeping his left arm round her, he moved with her away from the smouldering rush, and guided her across the dyke—lifted her, as she remembered it.

They seemed to have the whole of that shimmering day to themselves. Their walk to the withy bed was like a dream, whether a long or short one she never knew. When they stood among the young blossoming palm he stopped and began to stroke her hair again and kiss it softly. Then a man whistled and a dog barked quite close at hand. Jim Rounce took his arm quietly away, and called, " Is that you, George ? " One of the farm-hands answered, " Ay."

" All right, I'm coming," said young Rounce, and smiled at her and swung away. Elsie sat down on a tree-stump and leaned her back against another, looking at a slender limb of palm that went up delicately against the pure blue sky ; it was spotted to the tip with shining buds like silver pearls. Her heart was singing in her ears. She saw the beauty of the palm without wonder, all the purity of the spring colours, the pale primrose at her feet, the pearly buds against the pale blue sky, the dim Downs, the water-meadows full of flowers and fire and peaceful cattle—all without wonder She understood everything now.

When she got up, the heavenly blue was flushed with rose and saffron, with a clear stretch of greenish sky above it showing a daylit star or two. She was stiff with long sitting, but she did not notice it. She went without fear over the dykes with their unsteady bridges, without fear even through the grazing bullocks. She lingered here and there, gathering flowers and branches at random. When she reached the farm it was nearly dark.

" How late you are, child," said Miss Rounce.

"Aren't you famished for your tea? What have you been about?" Elsie laid down her handfuls on the window-seat "Oh, I see. Getting flowers and truck to take back with you. We'll set 'em in water overnight, and they'll be fresh for you in the morning. Don't you be too late abed. You'll have to bestir early."

"Never mind," said Elsie, "it's my last night. I don't want to think about the morning."

"Come and get your tea then. I've waited for you.

Elsie went over to the table and sat down, smiling and dreaming. She saw there were two places laid. "Where's Mr. Rounce?" she asked. "Isn't he coming?"

"He's had his. Wouldn't stop for more than a bite. It's the dance at Sparrow's, you know."

"Sparrow's? What dance?"

"The Bank-holiday dance—they always give one. There now, you ought to have gone, but they keep it up till morning, and it's five miles off—you'd never have been here for your train. There'd ha' been no getting Jim away to fetch you back. He's first to come and last to go when it's dancing. Besides, he's on his bike."

"Do you mean he's gone already?"

"Half an hour before you came in." As she spoke Miss Rounce bustled back and forth with pasties, eggs and cakes, butter and cream, and the apple-jelly Elsie could not resist.

"When is it——" Elsie stared at her, stopped and changed her question. "What time will he be back?"

"Dear knows," said Miss Rounce impatiently. "Best not to ask. I never do now. A man must go his own way. Here's your tea all ready. Set to, child. I'll have to tell Jim good-bye for you."

Elsie drank half a cup of tea, and pushed it from her.

"What's the matter?" said Miss Rounce.

"I'm so sorry," said Elsie. "Miss Rounce, I'm dreadfully tired. I do think I'll go to bed early, after all."

"Well, I think you'd better. But take your tea first, my dear."

"I don't want anything," said Elsie.

"That's nonsense, child," said Miss Rounce.

"I can't really," said Elsie, looking at her with her eyes full of tears.

Miss Rounce pretended not to notice them. "You've been doing too much," she said severely; "that's like all you Londoners—

FIRING THE RUSH

come down for a few days' rest and keep going from morning till night. Now you get up to bed, and I'll come along presently and bring you a night-cap."

"Please don't," begged Elsie. "I couldn't. I'll just get to bed and go to sleep."

"Well, it's the best thing you can do," said Miss Rounce. "I'll give you a call before five."

"Thank you. Good-night, Miss Rounce." Elsie went upstairs.

"Upset at going back to town," said Miss Rounce to herself. "That's what it is."

In her room Elsie gradually packed her small bag, and changed her frock for the everyday coat and skirt she would travel in. Then she blew out her candle and sat down by the open window, and watched the dim earth in the starlight and moonlight. She heard an owl hooting, and other birds that she did not recognise made croaking noises. The farm beasts moved and shuffled in their stalls, and once a cow lowed. Then they settled, and all outside was still. The clock struck ten. Miss Rounce came up to bed, and in a quarter of an hour there were no more sounds from her room. Elsie sat on at the window.

At a quarter to five Miss Rounce knocked on

her door. "I've brought you a jug of hot water," she called.

"Thank you, Miss Rounce," Elsie opened the door and took it in.

"Why, you're dressed already!" exclaimed Miss Rounce. "There was no call to be so early, you've plenty of time. You don't look as though you'd had a wink."

"I didn't sleep very much," said Elsie. "I did sleep a little, though. Is—— ?" She didn't finish her question. "Thank you for bringing this. I'll feel fresher for a hot wash."

"Breakfast will be ready for you when you come down," said Miss Rounce.

Elsie made her toilet, but still looked dragged under the eyes. She carried her little bag down with her, and while she breakfasted Miss Rounce did up her flowers in a basket with some eggs. Then Elsie went and stood at the door, and looked along the road in the cool sunless air.

"Worth won't be here for a few minutes, I expect," said Miss Rounce. "We're early."

But Elsie stood watching till the carrier's cart appeared. Then she turned to Miss Rounce and said, "Good-bye. And thank you ever so much for everything. You've been ever so good to me." And she kissed her.

The stout kind woman, who had got fond of

her, said, "Now don't you forget to come back to us some time or other."

Elsie smiled faintly, and climbed into the cart and was driven away.

"Bless us," thought Miss Rounce, standing at the door and waving her handkerchief, "she looks just as white as she did the night she come."

ANNA

I

LIGHT

FRIENDS were in the cottage that week-end, and Sunday was set apart for a picnic. But that was not the first thought in Anna's mind when she woke and saw the shaft of dewy sunlight on her whitewashed wall, and the flicker of leaves beyond her open window. Birds piped and darted in a way that told her it was still early. She looked at her watch ; it was a little before six.

She wondered whether she should try to sleep again. The morning was too sweet for sleep, and she was not sleepy, but she wanted the next hour to pass. She turned on her side and put her face into the pillow and lay still, playing with her thoughts. If you had asked her, " What are you thinking ? " she couldn't have told you ; but she could have told you of what she was thinking. Her thoughts went round and round without her will. Sometimes her face was smiling in the pillow ; now and then she suddenly pressed the pillow hard against her eyes, not knowing that she did so.

Her bed-head was beside the window, and the gentle movement of the air flowed across her cheek and neck. It called lightly, as the scent of flowers calls in the evening; it had to be answered, if only by a moment's pause. Anna turned and raised herself upon an elbow, and felt the air upon her face and breast; the sleeve of her nightgown fluttered. The birds were singing more steadily, less in detached notes and little calls. "Come out, Anna, come out, come out of it! Come out, Anna!" they seemed to be singing. She looked at her watch again. Five minutes had passed. The hour would never go like this.

She got out of bed and went to the cottage door in her bare feet. Her room was on the ground floor. All the other people in the cottage slept above, and none was stirring. Anna went into the garden in her nightdress, and walked along a grassy track where the blades stood up wet and crisp like little silver spears. The early light and air were as tender as childhood. Whenever Anna tasted this stainless quality of heaven and earth just after dawn she wondered at the many mornings when she missed it, let it pass untasted. She looked at the rosebushes to see what new roses had opened in the night, and stooped to shake the water from the blue cups of her Canterbury Bells. On she went, and picked a handful of red currants and ate them, first holding them up in the sun, strings of small shining jewels. When she came to the swing she sat down in it, as though this had been her purpose in walking down the garden ; she pushed with the ball of her foot against the earth and set herself in motion, but she let the single effort swing to its end unrenewed, and by the time the swing had ceased to move she was leaning her cheek on her arm stretched up the rope, and had forgotten where she was.

A man's step sounded on the path behind the hedge. Anna jumped up and went behind some bushes, and watched the garden-gate ; but the man went by, he was only a labourer going up to the farm. When he had disappeared, Anna walked back quickly to the cottage. It was still silent, and she began to wash and dress herself. Presently she heard the maid laying the kitchen fire. Anna brushed out her hair, and tried to decide what she would wear at the picnic. For some reason, or none, her heart had grown heavy ; the picnic did not matter very much. There was a little flowery dress she had never worn, but she wanted to save it for a special day—she didn't know what day. But for this day last year's frock would do.

Again a man's step sounded outside. This time it was the postman, and he turned in at the gate. Anna made a movement to meet him, but she heard the servant go to the kitchen door and receive the letters. The maid and the postman exchanged a few words, and soon he went away. Then Anna came out of her room and went into the kitchen. The letters lay on the table, and the servant had gone into the pantry. Anna turned the letters over rapidly, and took out two that were addressed to her. She had them in her hand when her younger sister came rather noisily down the kitchen stairs; she was in her dressing-gown, and her hair was in her eyes.

" Was that the postman, Anna ? "

" Yes."

" Anything for me ? "

" I didn't notice."

" Selfish pig. Who're yours from ? Oh, bother ! nothing, as usual. It's going to be a nice day."

" Yes," said Anna happily, " it will be beautiful for the picnic."

She went back to her room and finished doing

her hair. She did it very carefully, and she put on her flowery gown.

At breakfast, every one was in good spirits. Anna was happier than any ; she did not initiate, but she responded to, the talk and laughter with a quickness that made it seem her own. But she didn't know what she said, or what she was laughing at. She sat among her friends like a rose bathed in its own scent. Her left hand often touched her pocket under the table.

When breakfast was over there was a good deal of bustle. In the kitchen it took three people to cut sandwiches, one to slice, one to butter, one to spread the potted meat. Two more went to the garden to pull lettuces and radishes. One man volunteered to put up the drinks single-handed. Anna came by presently with a cabbage-leaf full of currants, and asked him smiling, " Are you done ? "

" Quite."

" Oh, where's your head ? " she laughed, and pointed to the corkscrew lying on the dresser.

" Is that what *you* open screw-top bottles with, young woman ? Where's *your* head ? "

" Oh, I don't know ! I thought you could open any bottle with a corkscrew." They both laughed, and helped themselves to currants. "Don't be too greedy," said Anna, "or I must pick some more."

"There are plenty, aren't there ? Don't you be lazy—or stingy, what's worse. I say, Anna, you rather fancy yourself in that dress, don't you ? "

"Yes, I know it's pretty," she smiled. ("And so are you," he thought.) "That's your last, now ! " She ran off with her cabbage-leaf. As soon as she had delivered it she slipped into her room for a moment and stood behind the door with her hands pressed together and her eyes shining. Somebody called her, and she answered, "Yes, coming ! " and ran back to the kitchen to help pack the hampers.

The pony-trap came to the door ; the baskets and three or four of the party were stowed inside it ; the other people had bicycles. Anna drove. The hand that did not hold the reins lay on her pocket. The young man who was responsible for the ginger-beer caracolled around the pony on his cycle, and tried to get the driver into difficulties.

"Anna, you're hopeless," he gibed. "Why can't you keep his head straight ? People in pretty frocks oughtn't to try to do anything more than sit with their hands in their laps and look ornamental. Think you can drive, don't you? Whirroo!"

"Stop it, or I'll run you down, I will really!" protested Anna. "*I* don't mind, but do leave my poor little beast in peace."

"All right—promise to sit in my boat and not ask to row, and I will."

"That's a bargain," said Anna; "I'll steer."

"Heaven help us!" groaned the young man, "that's done it!"

He careered down the hill.

"There's the river," said Anna to nobody in particular. "How beautiful it is looking to-day."

There were two boats at the river; Anna sat in the young man's boat, facing him. She let the girl beside her hold the lines, and trailed one hand in the water, plucking at water-lilies, when they came within reach. Just below the surface of the stream the bright goblets of the yellow lilies stood erect on their thick stems. Anna managed to snap off two or three, but lost her pleasure in them as soon as she had them in her hand.

"How disappointing they are out of the water," she said, and flung them away, turning her head to watch them drift behind her. The sun was dazzling on the landscape; in a haze of brightness she saw the yellow spots of the lilies, the purple of the loosestrife among the reedy banks, the gay cattle in the field beyond, and the blue and white of the sky. And she saw the ripple of the stream, the movement of clouds and grass, the shaking of aspen-leaves. She gazed until she ceased to see anything, but her thoughts swam in a haze of colour and motion. The rower wondered when she would turn her head.

"Regretting your lilies?" he asked.

"What? Oh, the lilies." She faced him again, in a kind of enchantment. The scene still danced a little in her sight, nothing was quite in focus. "No," she said, "I don't like the yellow ones. I want a white one. There's such a beauty."

"There is; but I'm not going to get stuck in the reeds even for you," he replied.

"I'd make a face at you if it weren't so hot," said Anna.

"You don't look hot," he said; she looked very cool and sweet under her shady hat.

"You do—poor you! And you won't let me row."

"I will not. D'you suppose I want to go back to London to-morrow covered with duckweed?"

"I don't suppose you want to go back to London at all."

"I don't."

Anna smiled at him.

"Anna's flirting," thought the girl with the lines.

The young man rowed in silence for a while.

Anna touched her pocket and went on smiling and trailing her hand in the water.

They landed somewhere and ate their lunch in a big meadow under an oak that stretched its branches over earth and water. Anna fetched things and passed things and forgot to eat.

"You've eaten nothing," said the young man, as the party began to scatter : "have a radish?"

"I'd rather have that water-lily."

"Tenacious young person. I'll get you some forget-me-not, if you like."

"I want that lily."

They walked by the bank awhile, and gathered flowers and talked, of what Anna hardly knew. Her hand went continually to her pocket, and once, letting her eyes drop, she secretly held it a little open, so that she could peep within. Once or twice she sent him from her side to get some spire of loosestrife or lovely tuft of meadowsweet. He would be gone but a moment, and then they would stroll on, chatting and laughing. Her sister and two or three of the others met them presently, and soon after when they looked for Anna she had disappeared; but before long they found her kneeling in the grass behind a tree, looking across the river.

"Dreaming of what?" he asked.

"Nothing in particular. The river, I think; the sun on it. Oh look! did you see that fish jump?"

"Wish I'd got my rod."

The hot day wore away. While the girls prepared tea some of the men bathed. Afterwards they washed the tea-things very leisurely and cleaned the knives in the grass, and then they got into the boats again and rowed back, singing most of the way. Anna was in the other boat this time. The young man was discontented, but to Anna the journey back was the same as the journey out—every instant of the day had been the same to her, alight and tremulous. The late sun shimmering on the water was like the shimmering of her thoughts.

She drove the pony as before. Her friend cycled beside the trap, but less exuberantly than in the morning. As they went along he cast something up into her lap. It coiled and touched her cheek before it fell; it was cold and clammy.

"Oh, a snake!" she cried, startled. Then she laughed.

"Your water-lily," said the young man.

"How stupid of me. But of course it's not *my* water-lily."

"How do you know?"

"Do you think I don't know my own lily?" said Anna.

"Well, take what the gods send you, anyhow, and don't be ungrateful."

"I beg your pardon," said Anna sweetly. "Thank you."

It was late when they got to the cottage. The pony was turned into the orchard, and they lingered about the garden for an hour. Somebody made cocoa, and whoever wanted bread and cheese fetched it from the larder. Anna's heart beat quickly. The day would soon be over. It had been a beautiful day, but she wished it to end; she wished to be alone in her room, in her bed.

The people went in one by one. Anna stood by the door of her room that opened into the garden. She leaned against the frame and looked up at the sky, trying to count nine stars.

Her friend strolled up.

"What are you doing?" he asked.

She told him.

"Why nine?"

"You get a wish then—but you have to count them nine nights running, and wish the same wish for it to come true. And you never do. It rains on the fifth night, or you forget on the eighth, or something."

"I've counted nine," he said.

"Have you made your wish?"

"Yes. Have you?"

"Yes."

"You look very happy, Anna."

"I am happy," she said. "Good-night."

"Good-night."

She gave him her hand. Her eyes were shining. He lingered, but she didn't move, so he went away.

Anna went into her room and turned the key. She drew the curtains and lit her candle quickly. She could scarcely wait. She had only read it once.

In another hour she was asleep, with her letter against her heart.

II

DARK

For a few moments after the train left the station Anna sat quite still, with her hands folded on her knees and her face composed, because of the other people in the carriage. She was conscious of two things—one, a buzzing of all her senses that came between her and external impressions like swarming bees, a faint intoxication, a sense of dream, blurring her hearing, her sight, and even her sense of touch. The other thing was a small void in her breast that threatened to increase and engulf her in vacancy. If it increased beyond a certain point she was sure she would slip over the edge of desolation, and perhaps not recover herself for weeks, or years, or a lifetime ; since the jerk back from despair to normal life needs a great spiritual effort. And at present her spirit was wandering helplessly somewhere among her memories of the past few days ; words and glances and gestures, words she was glad of, words she wished had been unspoken or spoken differently, small things that seemed to set irrevocable seals for good or ill upon undefined relationships . . . The hollow place in her heart swelled.

She looked up hurriedly to get in touch with something—to find some one to speak to or smile at, and by these mechanical acts suppress the thing she dreaded. If she could ignore the void long enough, if she could muffle it with assumed interests and occupations, she hoped it might be conquered. Presently, unfed by thought, it would shrink to the size of a pea ; just now it threatened to become as immense as the world, a world containing no life except her own. And then she knew she would be lost. She must not go adrift. She must continue to contain this void, she must not let it contain her.

A woman with a baby and a small girl sat opposite her ; beside the woman, her husband. It was the beginning of the yearly family holiday, and about the older people was a weak air of pleasure that grew vivid in the little girl, who occupied the corner seat, and kneeled at the window. On the same side, in the other corner, was a woman with an attaché case, which she opened frequently, busy with papers and pamphlets and a notebook, in which she scribbled intermittently. Her face was pale, tired, intelligent, and hard. In the fourth corner, on Anna's side, a friend of the writer was reading an article in one of the advanced reviews. She did not look so intelligent as the woman with the attaché case, but bore more evidently the stamp of belonging to some movement. Whatever the movement was, Anna put her down as a recent convert. From time to time she leaned across the carriage to make a comment on what she was reading, or to point out some passage with a significant look. Her comments, whenever they reached Anna, appeared unimpressive and were evidently so to the writer, who accepted them with a brief negative or affirmative. From neither of these women did Anna expect much help. She turned again to the holiday family. The baby was growing fretful. The mother quietly opened her blouse and began to feed it. Anna looked tenderly at the curve of the small head that had buried its features and its whole sense of being in the breast that was its world. The woman glanced at Anna, and they exchanged a smile. During that instant the emptiness in Anna was obliterated—not merely forgotten, but filled. She asked, " How old is he ? "

" Eleven months," said the woman, " and got eight teeth."

" He's a lovely baby," said Anna. " Are

you going to the seaside ? " she asked the child at the window.

The child nodded shyly.

" You'll make puddings and castles, won't you ? "

" Yes, and I'll paddle. I've got a Teddy Bear."

" You must let Teddy paddle, too."

" Yes, I must." The child looked pleased and surprised. " Mustn't I, mummy ? Mustn't I, daddy ? Teddy must paddle, mustn't he ? "

The father made a semi-jocular rejoinder under his breath, with a bashful glance at Anna, who did not hear what he said. But she smiled at him as though she had heard ; and suddenly felt tired, too tired to pursue the talk. The humming in her ears and eyes and nerves had come back in full force, and she could not clear a way through it to these people.

At the next station two sailors got in, big men, coarse and burly, and in loud spirits. They took the seats between Anna and the reader, mopping their faces and exchanging the kind of jokes that invite the attention of a strange company. The ladies in the corners buried themselves in their reading and writing. The family party listened with the surreptitious smiles which suggest inclusion. The men were vulgar, boisterous, and full of good will. Anna liked them, but felt it impossible to speak to them unconstrainedly, because of her preoccupation. At their entrance the mother had ended the baby's meal abruptly, and now the baby resented it.

"Fie, Gertrude!" said one of the sailors.

"Give 'er to me, ma," said the other, making a long arm across and grabbing the infant. "I got fourteen this size at 'ome. Wot I do' know about keepin' a kid quiet!"

"You'll be busy to-night, George," said his mate.

"Yus, if I'm lucky," said George with a wink. "Hi-yup, Gertrude! go fer 'im!" He shoved the baby, who was now perfectly happy, at his mate, and the baby clutched at a rose in the man's jacket, and tried to stuff it in its mouth. George checked it.

"Not so, Gertrude!" he said reproachfully.

"It's a boy," smiled the mother.

"Oh Gertrude! 'ow could you deceive me so?" cried the sailor. "D'you 'ear that?—it's a 'im not a 'er. Hi-yup, Julyun!" He thrust the baby once more at his mate, and then with appalling boldness at the lady with the attaché case. She took no notice. George glanced at her friend. "Better not!" he said, and continued to play with the baby and the rose. His movements were not gentle, but his large coarse hands must have been. He lurched the baby this way and that, but he always knew how to hold it, and was on guard at the slightest approach of the rose to the baby's mouth. Whatever misgivings the mother may have had to begin with were quickly appeased.

The second sailor began to fumble in his pocket.

"Does anybody 'ere———?" he said. Then he interrupted himself with extreme gravity. "Oh, but fust I better see 'oo I'm arskin'." He peered deliberately into Anna's face.

"Do you want to smoke?" said Anna.

"Would yer mind?"

"No, not a bit."

"You?—you?—you?—Thanks, then I won't say no. 'Ave one?" He offered his packet to Anna, and winked. She shook her head. She really didn't feel equal to him, and she could see that he imagined she was timid. He offered his cigarettes all round the carriage, knowing they would be refused. When he addressed the two ladies he nudged George openly.

"Where you gettin' out?" he asked Anna.

"Asham," she answered. She made an effort

to concentrate on him; she did not want to snub him, but could think of nothing better to say than, " Are you joining your ship ? "

" My ship ? *me* ? I aren't a sailor. I'm a insurance agent." He looked at her with an air of aggrieved reproof. He was exactly like a sailor on a music-hall stage. She could not rise to him and was silent, feeling that she had failed signally in repartee and disappointed an audience.

" Funny 'ow they goes fer a bit of colour," said George. The baby was fingering the red flags on his sleeve.

" Got any of yer own ? " his mate asked Anna, jerking his elbow towards the baby.

" I'm not married."

" Wot ? Then *I* shall get out at Asham." He grinned affably at Anna, and she smiled faintly, but he seemed to be a world away; and all this talk was happening between him and some girl she had never seen, and could not visualise. It was a common feeling with Anna when she talked to strangers. She knew that to them she was not Anna, but any pleasant girl; her personality was not concerned. Because of this, certain sorts of familiarity, and even insult, passed through her without touching her; they applied to her sex, not to herself. She was merely a presence being practised on by another presence, the sense of contact was wanting. Without the strange secret of intimacy, such intercourse was only the formula of puppets. In another mood she could have taken the sailor at his own valuation, and answered him. It would not be Anna answering, for what had Anna to do with this sailor, or what, indeed, the man under the sailor to do with the girl in the pretty hat who was just now a medium for his good spirits?

When she got out at Asham he opened the door for her and handed her her bag, saying, " Ah, well, friends must part ! " and she thanked him without smiling, because her abrupt vacancy of spirit was on her again. The sight of the familiar country she loved so deeply stirred all her loneliness in her. She had left it only three days before, eager and happy. And now she had come back to it, and the three days lay behind her. Yet, by such a small effort of imagination, the white road was the road of three days ago, and she the girl who had run to catch a train not due for fifteen minutes when she reached the station ; and the three days were before her, with all their possibilities. She had foreshadowed conversations and events as she longed for them to be, as she could *make* them be. And yet she had not made them, and had lacked the power to. Because on all the dreams which, in a friend's absence, fill out the life of friendship: on all the lovely silent talks and adventures : we have only the power to impress our own personalities. We use imaginatively the friend we love, and make him respond as we desire, or even, against our desire, as we think he would respond. And we have forgotten not only that part of his personality which acts for itself, but the irresistible and unforeseen reaction of this unknown quantity upon our own personality. So that not he alone, but we, act and speak otherwise than we have dreamed. Nothing that Anna had imagined had happened. Questions she had determined to ask had remained unasked. Things she had longed to tell had been untold. In thought she was courageous. But in fact she had been powerless; and she had struggled vainly to regain herself, a self which she knew existed in solitude, yet which under the unconscious influence of another spirit had been lost or changed past recognition. " Could I not have made the time lovelier, or happier ? " she thought as she went up the hill. " Did it have to be like that ? Couldn't I have changed it ? And is it really over ?—over ? "

She stopped to lean against a tree. Her heart

felt so empty, she thought in another moment she would sink upon the grass and weep and weep.

"I mustn't—— I *must not!*" she said aloud. She pulled herself up and walked quickly and steadily on. Some children were in the road ahead of her. She called to them gaily. "Hallo, Ethel! Alice!" The children came running.

"Hallo, Miss Anna."

"Where do you think *I've* been?"

"To Lunnon?"

"Yes, to London."

"Oh!" The children looked at each other quickly. Anna laughed.

"I don't know *what* you're thinking of."

"Got any sweets, Miss Anna?"

"Of course not! Look here, you tell all the others to come to the gate this evening, but you must give me time to unpack my bag."

"Yes, Miss Anna."

The children scampered off, screaming, "Sweets!" to the world.

Anna stopped at two cottages on her way, to talk to her favourite villagers. They were both hard-worked women, and both had come to an age when they felt their work. One was buxom, practical, warm-hearted, and garrulous; the other fragile and sweet and salty—she had the sweetness and the spice of herbs. Both were gossips, and their tongues did not always spare their best friends ; and both would have worn themselves ill for a neighbour in trouble, with less thought about it than a rich man's in writing a cheque for a charity. From these two women Anna heard all that had happened in her absence. They made her sit down ; and one who had been baking gave her a cake, the other, the little woman, a root from her garden.

"But what are you going to do then, miss ? " she said. " You'll find nobody at home."

"Nobody at all ? Did my sister go away, too ? "

"Yes, miss, yesterday, all of a sudden, and takes Lizzie with her. They wasn't expecting you back yet, she said."

"No, I came sooner—I wasn't expecting myself back. It doesn't matter, I can manage."

"What, in that lonely house, miss ? "

Anna laughed. "I don't mind being alone."

"Well, so long as it's not me ! "

Anna gathered up her flowers and went. It was a lovely evening, a sky like clear amber above

the ridge of the hills, and higher up masses of
lighted clouds lying motionless on the blue.
The serene light flowed from behind them upon
the downs with their rare crests of trees, and the
undulating slopes that moved in unbroken
curves, so smoothly were they spread with fields
of many shapes and colours. The heavenly
aspect of the hills and flats in the still light
caught at Anna's spirit with the mystery of all
beauty. The road had been too familiar ; but
light is as unfamiliar as the moods of the soul.
The land under that transfiguring sky was a
land Anna had never seen before, and she would
never see it quite like that again. Moved with
joy she entered the garden and let herself into
the deserted cottage.

She had expected greetings, tidings, questions
—to be responded to, listened to, answered and
disarmed ; she had been counting on the small
change of family life to stand between her and
her desolate breast. She had been prepared to be
forced to smile and seem cheerful and interested.
And there was nothing. No need to smile, no
need to conceal or assume. Her courage left
her. She ran to her room. From a slightly
open drawer hung the corner of a blouse she had
decided not to take in favour of another. She
had stuffed it back at the last minute. It might

have been but a minute ago. Was it, perhaps? Was she not about to start for the station? The room, just as she had abandoned it, was cruel in its suggestion. On the dressing-table was the telegram that had asked her to come. She caught it up and nearly pressed it to her lips. But Anna had pressed it to her lips three days ago. That was another Anna.

She threw herself on her knees by the bed, clasping her hands hard against her breast, to force that terrible void to contract within her. After a few moments she got up. She was trembling, but she had not wept at all. She was saying to herself, " You know there are things to do, and you must do them, if it's only to boil the kettle. You mustn't lose hold of yourself, you mustn't, you mustn't. You must make yourself do things quite regularly until you feel better. And you will presently. It doesn't last, it doesn't last. Something happens———"

She washed her face and hands, and tidied her hair, and went into the kitchen and put a kettle on the oil-stove. While it was heating she unpacked her bag methodically, and put her things away more quickly and neatly than was her usual habit. The village children soon came clustering round the gate; she chatted with them, teased them, gave them their sweets, and sent one of them for milk. Then she had tea, and collected her letters and mending. She sat on the hollow ache in her heart, and made her hands, and even a part of her mind, busy. But all the while, in a subconscious chamber of her spirit, she was re-creating things that had happened into things that might have happened, and creating, beyond these, things that still might happen.